REILLY

THE MCKEEGANS: A NEW GENERATION

BOOK TWO

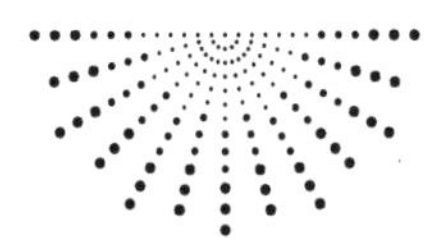

KATHLEEN BALL

❀ Created with Vellum

CHAPTER ONE

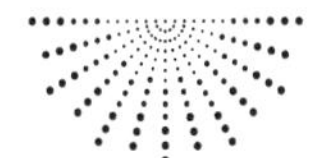

Reilly McKeegan tightened his grip on the steering wheel, his knuckles white against the dark interior of his car. Gravel crunched beneath the tires as the narrow dirt road twisted and climbed, trees casting eerie shadows under the moonlight. A sharp turn loomed ahead, and he slowed, his gut twisting with unease. Something wasn't right.

As the old secluded McKeegan ranch house came into view, Reilly's heart skipped a beat. The house was bathed in light, golden beams spilling from the windows onto the overgrown yard. The barn, too, glowed from within, as if hosting some strange midnight gathering. But no one was supposed to be here. No one had been here in years.

He killed the headlights and coasted to a stop. Silence enveloped him. Watching from the shadows, he scanned the property. Minutes passed, each second dragging, until something caught his eye. A figure darted from the barn, a flashlight bouncing wildly.

A woman. Alone.

Reilly's jaw tightened. He reached for the glove box,

cursing himself for not carrying his gun. The house was his, and he had no idea who this stranger was or why she was here.

Slipping out of the car, he approached the barn, his boots crunching softly against the dirt. Inside, a chorus of rustling animals greeted him—horses, some large bird, and... was that a llama? He ducked under the low beam of the doorway, and the intruder spun around, gasping.

"Who the hell are you, and what are you doing in my barn?" His voice came out sharper than intended.

The woman's eyes widened, her hand flying to her chest. "Reilly?" she whispered, her voice trembling. "Is that you?"

Recognition slammed into him. "Lynne Walsh?" His gaze swept over her, taking in the hay clinging to her jacket, the smudge of dirt on her cheek, and the defiant tilt of her chin. "What are you doing here? And what's with all the—" his eyes landed on two baby opossums curled up in a crate, "—wildlife?"

Lynne's mouth opened and closed. "I... I'm feeding them," she said finally, as if that explained anything.

"Feeding them?" Reilly folded his arms, his temper simmering. "In my barn? You've got some nerve, Doc. Care to explain?"

She lifted her chin. "I didn't know you were coming back. No one's been here in years."

"Does Stewart know you're here?" he asked, folding his arms in front of him.

"Well, not exactly."

"It's a yes or no question."

"I beg your pardon, counselor, no." She smirked.

"Well, I'm back now," he growled. "Finish up and pack your things. You're leaving tonight."

Her eyes flashed, and for a moment, he remembered the fiery woman who had once stolen his heart. "I'm not going anywhere until I've taken care of these animals," she snapped. "I'll leave in the morning. You can spare me that much, Counselor."

He opened his mouth to argue, but her words stopped him cold. The last place Lynne Walsh would willingly come to was the McKeegan ranch. Something was wrong.

"Lynne." His tone softened, though his frustration remained. "What happened? Why are you here?"

Her shoulders sagged, and the fight seemed to drain out of her. "It's a long story," she muttered.

Raising an eyebrow, he folded his arms and leaned against the door frame, waiting.

She shook her head. "Grandpa died, and he had a loan for the ranch. That means—"

"I know what it means. When your grandpa died, the house and land went to the bank. I would have thought being a veterinarian you'd have more than enough money to buy it back."

"You'd think so." She sounded bitter. "Grandpa had cancer and no insurance. I quickly signed him up for Medicare, but by then, the medical bills had already mounted. Plus, your brother refuses to allow me to come here on vet calls and word got around that he doesn't trust me. I only get calls for cats and dogs and not many of those to make a living."

Reilly sucked in a breath, needing to say something. Anything. But no words formed on his tongue.

She narrowed her eyes into a glare. "Don't you dare feel sorry for me! I have an opportunity to work for a vet in Billings."

He winced. Stewart hadn't allowed Lynne on the property out of principle.

"You did break my heart. But I'm sorry about your practice. Stewart didn't want you here because he was being loyal to me." He paused, tilting his head and studying her, noting the dark circles under her eyes. "He didn't explicitly say he mistrusted you, did he?

"No, but he waited on the phone for a half hour for West to take the call, even though I was standing right there. He made a big deal about refusing to talk to me. Small towns, you know?" Her smile didn't reach her eyes.

He hesitated, torn between sending her on her way and letting her stay. But the weariness in her eyes and the subtle tremor in her hands made the decision for him.

"Where is your pickup?" He frowned as he glanced around.

"I've been using the motorcycle." She released a deep sigh. "I'll just grab a few things before I go. It was nice to see you, and I promise to have all these animals out of here in a few days."

She put on a good act, but he didn't believe one word of it. The last place she'd have willingly come to was the ranch.

"Fine," he said gruffly. "You can stay the night. But we're talking in the morning."

Relief flickered across her face, and Reilly's chest tightened. He had a feeling letting Lynne Walsh back into his life was about to complicate everything.

IT WAS GETTING LATE, and the nighttime motorcycle ride down the mountain would be challenging. It had never occurred to her that Reilly would ever be at the house.

"I'll stay out of your way. I'll make a few calls in the morning, and then you should have the house to yourself," she said, hoping she sounded more confident than she felt.

"I'm sorry about your grandpa," Reilly said softly. "It must have been a hard time for you. Wasn't he the last of the Walsh family?"

"Besides me, yes. He only had one son, my father. He never got over losing my dad and my mother too, of course. He was kind to me, but you know all that. It was a bit shocking to find the house sold out from under me. I tried to get a loan to buy it back, but the land is worth more than I could ever afford." She lifted one shoulder, let it drop. "I'm a survivor, always have been. I have a few more animals I need to check over and feed. I'll meet you inside."

His eyes settled on her for a moment, then with a nod, he turned and walked out of the barn.

Relieved, she closed her eyes and leaned against a horse stall. It had been three years since she'd talked to Reilly. Every holiday she both hoped for and feared that she'd catch a glimpse of him in town, but it never happened.

If there was a way to get over the man she loved, she'd tried it. Dating others didn't work. Then she had tried online dating, and that had been disastrous. She had prayed, talked to the pastor, and one of the women in town had even given her an anti-love potion. It had gradually gotten easier to go for longer periods without thinking about Reilly. Removing him entirely from her heart, however, had proven impossible.

Upon entering the stall, she checked Spike's leg. His knee joint had been horribly inflamed, but the swelling was already coming down.

"Good boy, I bet you feel a bit better today, don't you?" A simple headbutt was all she needed as confirmation. She stood and left the stall, closing it behind her.

Now, what? She couldn't delay entering the house any longer. Would she be timid or courageous?

She squared her shoulders. Courageous. Approaching the house cautiously, she hesitated and then entered. It was surprisingly warm in the house. A fire blazed in the fireplace. She hadn't used it. She didn't want to run out of wood in case it got unseasonably cold. Reilly lounged in an overstuffed chair near the hearth.

"You look comfortable," she said.

"I like this old furniture. It sure is more comfortable than anything I have in my apartment," he answered, smoothing a hand over the chair's arm.

If only she weren't so aware of his stare. She turned her back toward him. "Would you like coffee?"

"I'll have tea. I know you like that better. At least you used to," he added.

"Still do. Tea it is."

After putting the kettle on to boil, she stood at the stove waiting. She couldn't think of anything to say to Reilly. It used to be so easy. They'd never had the need to say anything when they were together. But now, awkward silence filled the air.

She brewed some tea in a small teapot, poured it into cups and brought it to the table. A smile touched his lips as he accepted the offered cup.

Sitting in the chair opposite the one he sat in, she wished she wasn't so socially backward.

"How long have you been here?" he asked, his voice breaking the silence.

"Too long. Several days." She sighed. "I know I need to find another place, but I work in the clinic during the day and spend my nights here. I haven't had much time to look. I'm no longer a partner in the practice, so my salary has been cut by more than half."

He stiffened and sat forward. "What do you mean, you're not a partner? Didn't you have a contract?"

"Yes, however, my services weren't sought by any of the ranchers. My contributions are lacking. If I hadn't taken all these animals in, I would have left town. I have nothing left here except them."

"Like a wildlife preserve."

"I'd need a license to do that. They are my pets. My journey began when I adopted a rejected, injured horse."" She laughed. "It's getting late. I'm in the bigger bedroom, but I can move tomorrow."

"Don't worry about it. You can stay until the animals are situated."

Standing, she stretched then stepped into the kitchen and deposited her empty cup in the sink. "Good night."

CHAPTER TWO

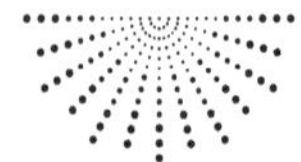

An uncommon quiet met Reilly when he woke up the next morning. He was accustomed to city noises; He got up and dressed. Was Lynne still sleeping?

Descending the steps, the quiet persisted. The cups from last night had been washed. She must have gone to work. His stomach sank at the thought of her predicament. Her grandpa had been a smart man. It was odd that he'd ended up with nothing.

Medical bills had bankrupted so many people. It was a shame. But it might be worthwhile for him to investigate the specifics. He shook his head. He'd be wiser to avoid involvement. The memory of her silent departure lingered with him. He'd thought... He released a sigh. It didn't matter anymore.

The house looked good. He had been skeptical, given the building's years of vacancy. He'd predicted that dust would be everywhere.

How significantly had they cut her salary? By more than half, she'd said. How could she afford to live?

Another sigh escaped his lips. He would inevitably

become involved. Hopefully, it wouldn't lead him down a path of hurt.

Wandering outside, he walked to the barn. Just how many animals did she have?

Three horses, a potbelly pig, two opossums, one mini horse, a hawk, and a wolf. A wolf? Really? She might have been like a crazy cat lady, but with a menagerie of animals.

How did she expect to re-home them? She couldn't possibly remain here. Daily contact with her would be too detrimental. He came here to regain himself not to allow an ex-girlfriend to stomp on his heart.

Stewart would be furious if he knew, even more furious at not knowing sooner. It was best to keep Lynne a secret for now.

Now what? He had no plan for self-discovery, or whatever people called it. He needed to reignite his passion as a lawyer. He was one of the best Billings—heck, the entire state of Montana—offered. He'd been approached about a political career more than once, but his love was defending people who were innocent.

Plenty of people hired him thinking they could fool him into believing they were innocent, but he'd always trusted his gut. He'd never been wrong until recently. Was it because she was beautiful? Was it because the evidence seemed preposterous? Maybe his anger at his client's mistreatment skewed his judgement. She'd just lost her whole family.

The fact that he lost the case didn't faze him. There was evidence he hadn't known about. Yes, they had withheld it, but it was inconsequential to him. His client was in jail where she belonged.

Now Lynne had appeared with a sob story. She had to leave.

Another cat with fleas. Lynne let out a sigh. The interns were seeing more interesting cases than she was. Her choice was gone; if she wished to remain, she had no voice. It wasn't a want as much as a need. She'd look at a few trailers after work and hopefully find a piece of land she could park it on.

It would have to be a used trailer. There were a few advertised in the paper, and she'd made appointments to see them later in the day. There would be no choice but to find someone to take her animals. She lacked the funds to provide both shelter and animal feed.

Maybe she was crazy, collecting unwanted pets. Well, not all were pets, but still, she should have walked away. She shook her head. She was incapable of walking away. Her stubbornness had gotten her in this mess. How would she get out?

There was a time when she felt on top of the world with a degree in veterinary medicine and a partnership in a clinic. The door opened. "Doc Lynne, your next patient is here. A new puppy checkup," the receptionist informed her.

She spent an hour that day riding to a trailer needing too many repairs, plus it had a big hole in it. She proceeded to the second one, after specifically asking its the condition. Since the seller of the first one had insisted it was in prime condition and the one she was on her way to was supposedly in fair condition, she was not terribly hopeful. Did it even have a roof?

As she drove closer to it, she caught sight of it and smiled. It didn't look as bad as the other one. Dared she hope?

A good-looking, physically fit cowboy greeted her after she got off her motorcycle.

A friendly smile was on his face, as he greeted her. "I'm

glad you showed up. So many people make appointments and don't show. Howdy, I'm Bob Harding." He put out his hand.

His handshake was warm and firm, but not too firm.

"It's nice to meet you, I'm Lynne. So, this is the trailer you're selling?"

"It is. Everything works. It was mine until my mother passed. I live in the house now. Come, I'll show you the inside."

He opened the door and gestured for her to go first. It was practically spotless. Would she be able to afford it? The stove and refrigerator looked new. No, it was probably too expensive. This one wasn't for her.

"It's nice, but I probably can't afford it. The amount listed in the paper must be a mistake."

"No mistake. I tried higher prices, but I didn't have any takers, and I'd really like to get it off my property. I'll need you to move it by Sunday."

"I don't have the land yet—"

A car drove by slowly and then backed up to a stop. Another prospective buyer. She'd need to decide now.

"It's a deal! I'll be here tomorrow to drop off the check."

A grin flashed across his face "You got it, Lynne. The check tomorrow and then moved by Sunday. You'll be happy with it."

"Thank you!" She got on her bike.

Now who was going to tow it for her and, most importantly, where was she going to park it? Paying for the trailer would wipe out her savings. But what other option did she have? Leave Tyrone and go where? She hadn't heard a word about the job in Billings. When she got back to the clinic, she'd call.

Had she jumped the gun by buying the trailer? If she got

the job, she'd be moving. Driving past her family farm, sadness washed over her. Word was it was going to be subdivided for tract houses.

Grandpa, I miss you!

The clinic parking lot was empty. That was odd. What was going on? She got off her motorcycle and walked to the front door. It was locked. A neatly handprinted sign on the door read "Closed for today. Under new ownership."

So, this was what it felt like to be gut punched. Who did something like this? Who kept the clinic staff in the dark about this kind of change? *David West, that's who.* If he'd sold the practice, he owed her money. Sure, she'd been taking a lessor role and had taken a pay reduction, but she had paid her way into the practice in the first place!

Her hands fisted as fury hit her. Turning, she saw West's car parked in front of The Morning Glory Café. He had the answers she needed. Marching over, she opened the door and stepped inside. It was as if she had tunnel vision.

She only saw West, who was laughing heartily, and strode over to the table. His laughter stopped abruptly.

"I think we should have a conversation," she informed him.

A smug smile played on his lips as he looked at her. "No, we don't. I've finally gotten rid of you."

Her face heated. "Excuse me? *Rid* of me?"

"Your reputation has gotten so bad, only old cat ladies will come into the clinic. I'm losing money because of you. We've all heard how you killed one of Stewart McKeegan's prize bulls. I should have let you go sooner." His gaze slid around the restaurant. "Perhaps you haven't noticed, but you're causing a ruckus."

Though her gaze remained fixed on him, her mind spun. *Killed a bull?* She glanced at the other restaurant patrons, most of whom were staring at her. West was correct about one thing; she was creating a scene. Huffing out a sigh, she turned on her heel and walked out the door, trying to appear fine, though she was certain no one bought her act.

It was definitely time to leave Tyrone.

CHAPTER THREE

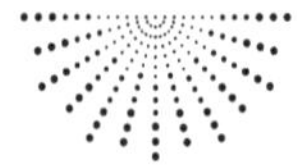

A tremor ran through Lynne as she approached Reilly's house, and she pulled to a stop where the driveway began. Dared she hope he was out for the day? Why did he want to live up in the mountains, anyway? There were other empty houses he could have chosen.

Dare she hope he was out for the day? Sighing, she climbed off the motorcycle and pushed it up the long drive. Maybe he wouldn't hear her.

Things hadn't been meant to get so complex. Marriage and a family had been within reach for her. She was foolish not to realize someone had been playing with her feelings. The scars of some hurts ran too deep to ever fade. Reilly's presence hadn't improved the situation. Even after three years, the memory continued to wound her deeply.

The house was lit up, dashing her hopes that Reilly was not home.

Usually, she changed into old clothes before working in the barn, but not today. Going straight to Spike, she accepted his head-butt and rubbed his nose. At least someone was happy to see her. "You seem chipper. I hope that means your leg is healing more."

Walking past two more horses, Paint and Bay, she gave each a rub on the forehead.

Paint's back bore so many scars, and when she'd found him, he had open wounds. Someone had used a crop on him. It had taken a while to get him to trust her.

Bay was pregnant with twins. Survival for the mother and foals didn't have the greatest odds. The owner had planned to sell her to a slaughterhouse.

Mini raced to the stall door, and Lynne laughed softly. "Happy to see me?" A supposedly grumpy and nasty miniature horse, Mini turned out to be sweet as sugar when Lynne got to know her.

The potbelly pig had been left on the clinic doorstep. West wanted to call animal control, but she adopted her instead. "How are you today, Tuni?"

Spitten, the llama, was next. The llama had walked down the center of town one day, and no one claimed him.

She'd named the opossums This and That. She couldn't tell them apart. When they were a bit older, she'd release them.

The wolf was Lucky. He'd been shot and left to die. She'd found him on McKeegan land. He'd be healed up soon.

Then there was the hawk. She'd named him One Wing, but soon she'd have to change it to Two Wings. He was healing nicely.

What was she going to do with them all? The horses would be sold and killed. She'd tried to find Tuni a home, but no one wanted a pet potbelly pig.

She cleaned their stalls and then fed and watered them. It was a project born of passion, and it was killing her inside to consider their fates now that she could no longer help them.

The metallic clatter of rain against the roof broke her reverie. The bike! Running out into the deluge didn't faze her. The motorcycle was about all she had left unless she counted the trailer that was about to deplete her bank account. She was soaked in seconds as she pushed her bike into the barn, but she ignored her discomfort and began to dry the motorcycle. Sometimes it didn't start as well after a storm.

A LIGHTNING STRIKE illuminated the dark sky, quickly followed by a rumble of thunder that made the house tremble. Surely Lynne would stay in the barn, wouldn't she?

He broke into a smile and chuckled. She didn't have enough sense not to start a zoo in the barn. He peered out the window, watching as another lightning flash brightened the surroundings. Movement caught his attention. What was she doing with her motorcycle? Why couldn't she just have stayed in the barn?

Against his better judgement, he put on his raincoat and Stetson and then made a run for it. He entered the barn as another tremendous boom rattled the earth.

"What are you doing here?" she asked. She was busy wiping down the motorcycle.

"Just checking on you. The storm is bad."

She nodded. "The lightning strikes sounded close. But I always enjoy thunderstorms. I feel a unique sense of aliveness when I am in them."

Reilly smiled. "I remember. So, how is the zoo today?" He walked over to the llama, and the contentious animal spit on his raincoat. "I forgot about the spitting." He removed his coat.

"That's why his name is Spitten." Her smile was wide and her eyes full of mischief.

"A fitting name." He pointed at the pig. "What did you name this animal? Piglet? Bellybutton?" He couldn't keep his lips from twitching.

"Of course not! That's Tuni, short for Petunia." Pausing in her wipe-down of the motorcycle, she made a face. "What's so funny?"

"Nothing. What about the short horse? Shortie perhaps?"

"You're making fun of me. That is Mini, and before you ask, the opossums are This and That, The hawk is One Wing and the wolf is Lucky. The horses are Spike, Paint, and Bay. Any questions?"

"Spike?"

"He had a spike in his hoof. This and That—I can't tell them apart. One Wing only has one wing working. The wolf was shot and, well, Paint and Bay are self-explanatory." She narrowed her gaze.

A booming thunderclap caused her to jump.

"Exactly how long have you called this home?"

"Long enough to have put the utilities in my name. I just need a little while longer." She released a sigh. "Oh, and I got fired today."

"Fired? How?" West couldn't just fire her.

"The door to the clinic was locked, and I saw West's truck outside The Morning Glory, so I went and asked him about it. He said he sold the practice. My reputation was driving his clients away. He also accused me of killing Stewart McKeegan's prize bull, a fact seemingly known to everyone." Another sigh escaped her lips; she looked deflated.

"I've never heard about a dead bull."

"I was hearing about it for the first time." She settled down on a bale of hay. "I had just enough money for the trailer, but I'll need to move it, and— Never mind, it doesn't matter."

"It does matter. If he sold the practice, he owes you

money from the sale. Did you sign any other contract when he started paying you less?"

"No. But I was distraught over Stewart and his ability to ruin my career. I felt lucky to have a job." Her eyes grew moist with unshed tears. "Then Grandpa died. You know the rest. I did have a lead on a job in Billings, but I foolishly put West down as a reference. Now it's clear to me why I didn't receive a call back."

"Lynne—"

Her hand went up. "This is my problem. I've been independently solving problems for quite some time. I don't need rescuing. I assure you, I'm not interested in your family's wealth or reputation. My greatest desires were to be loved and have children. I wanted a veterinarian practice." She stood up. "Since I don't have any of those, I have some things to figure out. Thanks for not kicking me out, Reilly. Good night. She ran out into the rain without a jacket.

He kept watching her until she got inside. He sensed something was amiss, and now more than ever, he was determined to uncover the truth.

CHAPTER FOUR

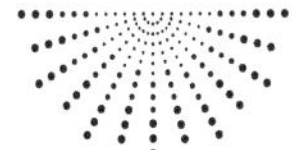

Waking up earlier than Reilly wasn't difficult. He clearly wasn't on ranch time. After feeding the animals, she rode to town. She would arrive just as the bank opened. Maybe it was crazy getting the trailer before the land.

Scatterbrained, she was definitely scatterbrained. She tucked the check into her purse and walked to the grocery store, Daily Provisions. They sold much more than groceries. But all she wanted right now was a newspaper.

Betty Wilkins approached her from behind as she was paying for the paper.

"We'll be thrilled once the new clinic is done. With so much land, we'll be able to have a barn for horses. Do you know when it'll be finished? West paid us for the next four weeks." A smile graced Betty's face. "It's a good thing, right?"

Betty always had such a positive attitude toward life.

"It's a good thing." Lynne offered a quick smile then made a hasty exit. She knew exactly where West planned to build his new clinic. On her grandfather's land. He'd heaped insult upon insult on her. Was he aware of the pain it caused? Probably. But he showed no concern.

Brushing away a tear, she hopped on her bike. The quickest route to the McKeegans led across her grandpa's property. Unwilling to do that, she chose the longer path.

The heartache grew stronger with each passing minute. What bull was Stewart McKeegan accusing her of killing? She'd thought he didn't want her on his property due to the way she and Reilly had broken up. Somehow, Stewart had placed the blame on her. He held grudges, but she doubted he'd fabricate a story about her and a bull.

Reaching the driveway was such a relief. She could restrain herself no more. Removing her helmet was all she could do before collapsing. There were hurts and then there were heart-wrenching, deep hurts.

She managed to get off the bike and grab the newspaper. Going into the house wasn't an option. Reilly couldn't see her like this. She'd rather ride out of town than see pity in his eyes.

She went into an empty stall, sat in the corner, and wept. One good cry and she'd figure out a solution, she promised herself. She erupted in a torrent of sobs. One good *long* cry. Then she'd be fine.

She'd lost everything she once possessed. She'd have to call and cancel the purchase of the trailer. Her sparse belongings would be boxed and sent to her new home upon her arrival. She could take enough in her backpack to get her by until then.

"Lynne?"

If only the earth could swallow her. Her face was most likely red and swollen. She hastily dried her eyes, using her sleeve.

"I'm in here."

As the stall door opened, his worried expression nearly caused her to cry again.

"I'm just reading the paper," she told him. Her attempt at cheer failed; she knew he wasn't deceived.

He hesitated a moment, then sat down next to her.

"I'll take a section, if you don't mind. I bet reading in here is peaceful." He held out his hand, and she handed him the sports section.

HE LEANED back against the stall wall and opened the paper. He pretended to read it.

"Must be a bad day for news," he mentioned, trying to sound casual.

Out of the corner of his eye, he saw her stiffen. He turned the page and stared at the paper some more.

"Do you want to share the news with me?" Sounding sweet was not his forte. He much preferred questioning witnesses on the stand. Straight forward, to the point, aggressive even.

She was silent for so long, he thought she wasn't going to answer.

"Things just aren't— I don't know. I found out a few things in town I didn't know, is all." She avoided making eye contact with him.

"Sometimes going into town isn't all it's cracked up to be. I mean, you might get gussied up and expect a fun time, but it isn't fun." Where was he going with this?

"I wasn't expecting a fun time." She stared at the paper again.

"How can I help?"

With a sigh, she folded the paper and placed it beside her. Her eyes were so puffy from crying.

"West bought my grandfather's land. He plans to build a clinic there. I'm so stupid. I thought he sold the practice, but he didn't. He lied to me. He's taken every single thing that was ever important to me. I went to the clinic daily, completely unaware of what was happening. I'm a good vet, Reilly. I really am. I wasn't even on this ranch when the bull died. It's just been one thing after another, and I'm sorry I'm a crying mess."

He slid closer beside her, wrapped an arm around her, drawing her into a hug. He'd rather be talking to—no yelling at—West, but Lynne needed him. A jolt shot through his heart. The last time she'd been in his arms was little more than three years ago. She'd left him and then blocked him. It had cut deep.

"Lynne, you can take your time moving out. You don't need added stress now."

Pulling away, she gazed into his eyes. "I bought a place, but I need help."

Bought a place? He schooled his features into a neutral expression. "What can I do?"

"I bought a trailer, and, well, I don't have anywhere to put it." Quickly, she glanced away.

"There's more. What is it?"

"I need someone to move the trailer before Sunday onto land I don't have. I don't know what I was thinking. Well, actually, I thought if I did everything one step at a time—"

"You? Not plan ahead? I mean every little detail."

She winced. "I'm not like that anymore. My life isn't like that. Being a vet has changed me. I had to learn to roll with changes. I do admit this move has been done in a panic. I mean, I needed a place to live and there isn't anything in town. I figured I could rent land, but the seller of the trailer wants the money today."

"Were you even planning to stay in Tyrone?"

"No, that's why I bought the paper. I need to find land to rent. If I didn't see anything in the paper, I was going to ask to use your computer."

"I have plenty of land, and you can be near your zoo—" His lips kicked up into a lopsided smile. "I mean animals. I'll arrange for the trailer's transport here, and I'll call a couple of people to get you hooked up with electricity and water. Nothing permanent, of course. It'll give you plenty of time to figure out what you want to do."

She awkwardly hugged him, and he gently kissed the top of her head.

"I need to wash my face and then go pay for the trailer. I'll be back this afternoon." She stood and brushed hay off her jeans. Turning, she faced him. "Thank you from the bottom of my heart." In an instant, she was gone.

He pondered her situation and the rumors surrounding her. A dead bull? He didn't remember seeing anything on the ranch financial statements about a dead bull. There were livestock losses all the time, but a prized bull would be accounted for in the financials. He frowned. He needed to talk to his brother, Stewart. None of this made sense. Stewart didn't want Lynne on the ranch because of how she broke things off. He was just being the protective brother.

There were some missing pieces of information.

CHAPTER FIVE

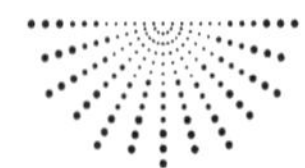

Reilly strode up the stone walkway to the house he'd grown up in. Stewart lived there now with his wife, Aurora. They seemed happy enough.

The door opened to reveal an elderly woman, her cheeks rosy, her hair white. He'd missed her welcoming smile more than he had realized until just this minute.

"Flora, good to see you. Is Stewart around?"

"He's in his office. Go on, I'll bring you coffee." She walked to the kitchen.

The house was one of the bigger houses on the ranch. Their branch of the family came down from Aiden McKeegan. There were six parcels of land. One for each of Eion McKeegan's sons. The ranch itself, however, was legally protected from division or sale.

Stewart stood when Reilly walked into his office. After shaking hands, Reilly sat in a plush chair facing the large desk.

"I didn't know you were coming home," Stewart said.

Reilly snorted. "My successful court case was overshadowed by the later discovery of my client's heinous guilt. I was slightly staggered by it and needed to get away from the city. I'm up at the house on the mountain."

A frown creased Stewart's brow. "That one is so secluded."

Reilly smiled. "It is exactly what I was looking for. I need to be alone for a while, but a bit of business came up, and I have something I need to discuss with you."

Stewart scratched his chin. "Sure. What's up?"

"Which bull did Lynne kill?"

Surprise flickered across Stewart's face. "Lynne didn't kill a bull. We did have one die. It was Thor, the one I purchased three years ago. He died out in the pasture, and West took care of getting him buried. Lynne hasn't set foot on this ranch."

"Lynne and I—that's all in the past—"

"You've seen her!" Stewart said, his eyes narrowing.

"Yes, it wasn't planned. West forced her out of their partnership without compensation or proper paperwork. Having sold his vet clinic, he is now building a much larger one on land that belonged to Lynne's grandfather. How the land came to be in his possession, I have no idea. In The Morning Glory Café, he created a commotion, blaming Lynne for your bull's death. He told her that was why the clinic was losing all its business."

"Here's your coffee, Reilly." Flora set it on the desk in front of him.

"Thank you, Flora," Reilly said, accepting the mug.

"I don't suppose you have coffee for me?" Stewart asked with a hint of a smile.

"Only on your birthday." She grinned and walked out of the office.

Reilly laughed. "She hasn't changed."

"Are you sure West is behind this? I had no knowledge of his plans. Has the new building opened yet? Now that I think of it, Lynne's grandfather had money. Didn't he? She must have inherited the land. Or could there be a relative we're unaware of?"

"I don't know. I'm going to investigate this. On the day Thor passed away, were you there?"

"No, I was told by McKenna that the bull was dead, said he'd called West and he'd take care of it. I was stuck in the office most of the day." Stewart sat back in his chair. "Incidentally, I wonder why McKenna's sentence was so significantly reduced. Do you know anything about that?"

Reilly considered their brother, who had a tendency to find trouble, and sighed. "Though I lack details, it seems he informed on the individuals responsible for placing drugs in the shed. I know he was responsible for introducing you to Paul Stingster. After Paul scammed the money from you, McKenna was to receive half. Unfortunately, Stingster's statement is unreliable and can't be used as evidence in court." He shrugged. "Don't know much more, but I'll make a few calls next week."

Reilly took a sip of his coffee. "I didn't see death of the bull on the financials. Shouldn't it have been on there?"

"It's tricky. We started the semen AI program a few years back. Artificial insemination."

A wry smile tugged at his lips. "I know what AI means."

Stewart nodded. "Thor commanded a high price per straw due to his superior genetics and high production. The depreciation on Thor ended. He was no longer considered an asset. But the death does need to be noted due to the loss of income from the AI program."

"In other words, you have the accountants figure it out."

"Yes, I don't want to get lassoed in that mess. Anyway, it'll be on the year-end statement."

"So instead of getting paid from another rancher to rent a

stud… never mind, I'm way behind on the technology of ranching."

"Was there any more business we need to discuss?" Stewart asked.

"No, little brother, but I have some things to investigate. How's married life?"

A contented smile spread across Stewart's face. "Couldn't be better."

CHAPTER SIX

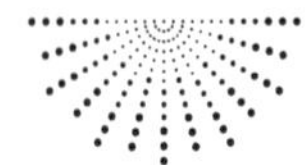

With the trailer purchased, uncertainty relentlessly swirled within Lynne. She should have had a contract or something. What if the trailer wasn't still there on Sunday? What was the matter with her? She was typically organized.

Reilly was being generous, allowing her to park the trailer on his property, but she didn't want to be beholden. A negative recommendation from West would severely impact her job prospects, though, and it might take time to find employment. If only her grandfather were still alive. He'd been her only solace when she had been told Reilly never wanted to see her again.

She'd have to lean heavily on her faith. She'd always gotten through doing that. She smiled. "It is what it is."

The rain started when she was about a mile from her destination, Reilly's house. She'd be soaked by the time she rode up that driveway. The rain pounded down, making puddles that ran across the road. If she didn't take care, she'd crash, so she slowed down. The rumble of a truck came from behind her, and she waved for it to pass her.

When it roared by, it simultaneously forced her off the road, throwing her down the embankment and into the sticky mud below.

For a minute, she didn't move. One by one, she checked to make sure her extremities were still working. Upon assessing no damage, relief washed over her. But she was pinned beneath the heavy bike.

Pushing it up the best she could, she scooted out a bit and then repeated the process until she was free from the motorcycle. Just her luck. Why the truck hadn't made a wide berth around her was puzzling. It was probably due to the rain.

Now all she had to do was lift her bike upright, somehow get it up the embankment, and ride home. The only way to get through a hard situation was to just do it. It took a lot of strength and jaw gritting before she finally got the bike upright. Pushing it up the hill was a no-go. It was a tiny hill, but it was impossible to push.

Maybe she could just try to ride it up and get back on the road. *Bike, please start.* She laughed when it started on the first try. Nothing ever sounded so good as the engine roaring. The bike, however, slipped on the hill. She scanned her surroundings. Riding in the gully seemed to be the best bet.

A warm bath, hot chocolate, tea, and soup. All the warm things she'd have soon. After riding through the mud for a while, she finally had enough speed to get the bike up onto the road, right where the turnoff for the driveway was.

By the time she got to the barn, she was soaked and covered in mud. But she was home. *No, don't think of this place as home.* That would only end in heartache. Unbearable pain. Once was enough for her.

The sound behind her caused her to jump. There stood Reilly, with an umbrella over his head, carrying towels. He put down the umbrella and unrolled the towels. A change of clothes was bundled inside.

"Hurry, you're shaking," he urged as he handed the pile to her.

Taking the clothes, she stepped inside an empty stall and dried herself. Thankfully, most of the mud was contained to her clothing. But she was shaking, it was so cold. Even the dry clothes didn't help much. She walked out of the stall, and Reilly instantly put his jacket on her. He hoisted her up and over his shoulder, picked up the umbrella, and quickly walked to the house.

He set her down on the chair closest to the fire, put on another log, and then he went into the kitchen. He came back out and handed her a cup of tea.

Tears filled her eyes. It had been a long time since anyone had shown her such care.

"Thank you. I appreciate all you do. I'm really an unnecessary nuisance." Pulling her legs up, she snuggled into the chair.

It was as though he could read her mind. The next minute, he placed a blanket over her.

"Can't have you getting sick," he said. He sat in the chair nearest to her. "You're still shaking."

"Yes, but less than I was, thanks to you." She smiled at him. "I paid for the trailer."

"I figured as much. I arranged to have it hauled up here and have the water, sewer, and electrical hookups connected. Now skirting was mentioned as something you'd want, but I figured that would be up to you. You can use my internet. They'll do it tomorrow."

A massive weight was lifted from her shoulders. "I don't know how to thank you. I've been so alone with no one to turn to. I won't make a habit of it, though. I promise. And of course I'll pay rent."

"We don't need to get ahead of ourselves. Let's just get you settled and see about the animals."

"See about the animals?" Did her heart just stop?

"There's plenty of land that goes with this house. You could expand. I'm not sure if there is much call for a place for hurt llamas, though." His grin warmed her.

"You'll leave soon, won't you?"

"I don't know how soon. I still have some things to work out. I did speak to Stewart about the bull. Its name was Thor."

She laughed. "Original."

"Stewart knows you were never there. He never saw the bull. West and McKenna disposed of it."

"Then why did he drag my name through the mud?"

"Because of me. He was just circling the wagons. I didn't take you leaving me well. I started drinking and fighting. I almost didn't go back to my last semester of law school." He looked sheepish, with his head bowed.

It was almost too much to take in at one time. Stewart never told the world she killed his bull. Bigger than that though, Reilly thought *she* left *him*. She opened her mouth to ask him about it.

"You look exhausted." He stood and held out his hand. "Let's get you to bed, and we'll talk in the morning."

CHAPTER SEVEN

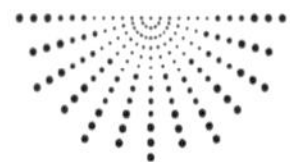

Staring into his cup of coffee, Reilly shook his head. He had been unaware of his desperate need to hear her say she hadn't abandoned him, or even being sorry for leaving without a goodbye. Heck, just some explanation.

It had been a week before he was to leave for his last year of law school. He'd split his summer into two parts. Time working on the ranch and time with Lynne. He had planned to propose before they both left for their final year of college. She was going to be a veterinarian.

Lynne informed his mother that she no longer wanted anything to do with him. That was it. No explanation. She didn't return his calls or texts. Then she blocked him. Her grandfather seemed just as confused as to why she suddenly left for school early. He did say she was visibly upset.

Any time Reilly questioned his mother, she just told him he was better off. But he hadn't been better off. He was so haunted by it that he could no longer trust women. He dated a few times, but none of them were Lynne. And as much as she had devastated him, he still wanted her.

So he had thrown himself into being the best lawyer he

could be and earned many accolades in Billings. He only came back home when something happened, such as his brother McKenna turning into a low life thief and drug pusher. He hadn't wanted to take the chance that he'd run into Lynne. It had just been easier to stay away.

It had been difficult seeing her here in the mountain house. His traitorous heart still beat for her. Repeatedly, he attempted to control his feelings, yet failed every time. He did have a great poker face that he had perfected in the courtroom.

Why, why, why had she thrown him away? She'd loved him. He hadn't been mistaken about that one fact.

And now...what to do about it all was on his mind.

He'd get her settled and then go after West. West had a lot of explaining to do. On top of that, he needed to find the source of the rumor of the dead bull. The fact that West accused her of having something to do with it at The Morning Glory was his best clue.

The truck hauling the trailer honked its horn as it came up the drive. He'd best stop all this musing and go outside.

Lynne's rosy smile of excitement instantly captivated him. She clearly had a sense of accomplishment over acquiring the trailer.

"I'll show you where to put it!" he yelled up at the driver.

Her own home. No one could kick her out except... She'd have to see Stewart and let him know she was living on McKeegan property. She had Reilly's blessing, and that was all that mattered, but having Stewart's blessing would mean she didn't have to practically hide. It would be awkward if he just happened upon her and the animals. Especially if he really blamed her for killing his prized bull.

Lynne found herself panting as she followed Reilly; he sure did walk fast. It was futile to try to catch up to him. She eyed the trailer being towed in, knowing she owed him her gratitude. He'd come through for her when he didn't have to.

The air crackled with excitement as she urged, "Reilly, look!"

"It's practically brand new," he marveled. "How's the inside?"

"It looks barely lived in. I can't thank you enough." Tears welled in her eyes. "But...I *will* need a lease. I don't want anyone to be able to make me leave."

"Who would make you leave?"

"Your mother," she managed to choke out. "I can't talk about it now, it makes me cry, ugly cry." She took his hand. "Come on, they have it situated. Let's look inside."

His nod and light hand squeeze were such a relief.

She climbed the few steps, opened the door, and went in. With pride, she gestured for Reilly to follow her. "What do you think?"

She smiled as he looked around. He even opened the refrigerator and oven. Then he stepped into the bedroom and nodded his approval at the bed and dresser.

"I think you got a great deal. I imagined it to be smaller. It's like a house. Nice of them to leave some furniture. You can borrow some sheets from the house to make up the bed."

"Thank you," she whispered. "For everything."

"I'm impressed, and yes, I will draw up a lease agreement. It's time we let Stewart know. Rent checks will go to him. Why are you looking at me like that? I'll go with you."

"I need to do this myself. I appreciate the offer, though. Tomorrow should be soon enough."

The front door burst inward, and Stewart pushed inside.

Lynne sighed. *Speak of the devil...*

"What the devil are you doing, Reilly?" Stewart bellowed,

staring around the trailer. His jaw dropped for a moment as he stared at Lynne. "Really? Reilly, I don't think this is wise. Have you forgotten what she did to you last time?"

She hesitated, giving Reilly time to defend her, but he didn't utter a word. She dashed out the door and into the barn. Clinging to a stall door, she gasped for air. *What* I *did?*

After stepping inside and closing the stall door, she slid down into clean hay. *What did I do?* Had Reilly told his brother *she* had broken up with *him*? Tears threatened, but she refused to allow them to fall, even as she remembered his mother's cruel, scathing words. She had recited so many reasons why Lynne would never be allowed to marry Reilly. And then she casually mentioned the fact Reilly had a lady friend at school. That had been enough to make her pack up and run.

Thinking she could live here had been a huge error. Her original plan of leaving town was the better one.

CHAPTER EIGHT

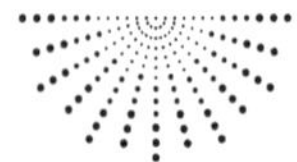

"It seems she's unable to acknowledge the truth regarding her actions," Stewart noted.

Despite his inner turmoil, Reilly nonchalantly shrugged at his brother. "It's been a long time and I'm sorting out what happened with West, her grandfather's land, and the bull."

"This isn't the place for her," Stewart maintained.

"I claimed this house and the land adjacent," Reilly said through clenched teeth. "She's paying rent to the ranch. It'll be fine."

A frown creased Stewart's brow. "Mother always said Lynne would be the end of you. She knew from the first date."

"I don't remember Mother's disapproval of Lynne," said Reilly. "Why didn't she speak to me about it?"

"Because you are hardheaded. She knew if she told you to stop seeing Lynne, you'd hold on to that girl tighter." Stewart gestured toward the door Lynne had fled through. "She left you in the end. Mother was right about her." Heaving a sigh, he seemed to deflate a bit. "But for your sake, I'll be civil. And when the family asks about her, and you know they will, I'll say it's fine." Shaking his head, Stewart gave Reilly no time to respond before he left the trailer, entered his truck, and sped away.

Reilly stared down the driveway long after Stewart's truck was out of sight, thinking as he ran his hand over his face. Lynne had received no dinner invitations, that was for sure. Mother usually invited everyone around. How had Mother known that Lynne would leave him?

Where had Lynne gone when she'd run out on him and Stewart? Sighing, Reilly walked to the barn and stood outside the stall where He'd found her crying last time. He had never recovered from Lynne's desertion, and reopening that old wound would be incredibly painful. But his gut was telling him they needed to talk and clear the air.

Lord, please allow me to be patient and not come undone. I need to control my anger. Amen.

After a deep breath, he opened the door, prepared to find her weeping again. When he found her sitting in the stall, instead of sorrow or remorse, she glared at him with clenched fists.

"What was that all about? You told your family I left you? Heck, you didn't even have the decency to break up with me in person. Sending your mother to have 'a little talk' was the cruelest thing you could have ever done." She paused and drew a deep breath. "Did you think it funny sending me texts after sending her to see me? Receiving those voice messages was excruciating; it felt like pouring salt on a wound. I almost didn't go back to college. I didn't think I could handle it. But Grandpa cautioned me against allowing you to steal my future. So I went back to school and got my degree." She took another breath. "I grew to hate you."

Reilly was reeling internally. It was difficult to absorb it all. He almost couldn't. His mother? Oh no, she could be biting when she wanted to. Her sharp tongue could strip the skin off a man from twenty feet away.

Though he wanted to walk out, Reilly seated himself beside Lynne, maintaining a respectful distance. "I didn't know. I swear. All I knew was you stopped texting me, you stopped taking my calls, and then you blocked me. You blocked me on all social media accounts." He took a deep breath. "I went to see your grandfather, and all he said was you left. He didn't treat me very kindly. He refused to answer any questions."

He fixed his eyes on the stall's aged wooden planks. Has his mother really done something so heinous? Sure, she could be meddlesome, but never anything like what Lynne had described. At least he didn't know of any other time she'd done something so malicious. But what if she had?

LYNNE STOLE A GLANCE AT REILLY. His face, etched with misery, nearly stopped her heart.

"I wish this was a romance novel and we could just forget it and run to each other in slow motion and rekindle our love." A smile tugged at her lips as the vision took hold. "You'd pick me up and my dress would swing around."

"I suppose the dress is important," he said with mock seriousness.

"Of course, and the air would smell like roses." Sadness rolled over her. "That was our life, and we were manipulated. I spent most of my first year crying myself to sleep. I tried to hate you, but I didn't even get close. I hardened my heart against you. After I graduated, West invited me to join his practice. Grandpa gave me the money." She sighed. "The first year was great. I had plenty to keep me busy, and I didn't mind being on call most of the time. Halfway into my second year, it got around that Stewart wouldn't allow me on the ranch. People treated at me differently. They seemed to be looking down on me. With Grandpa gone, I was forced to vacate the premises. I found a place above Gus' garage. You remember Gus, don't you? He owns half of The Morning Glory Café. My salary dwindled; the outcome was obvious."

"What did she say to you?" He practically growled.

With a shake of her head, a sad smile graced her lips. "I'll tell you another time. I think we were both played for fools. I have so much to think about. I'm glad we're friends. We are, aren't we?" She held her breath, waiting for his reply.

He reached his hand over and covered hers, giving it a small squeeze. "Yes, we are friends. And you're right. I have a lot to think about." He stood and brushed the hay from his jeans. "Need any help moving in?"

"No. I don't have much. I have clothes and that's about it." She stood. "I'd best get to it."

CHAPTER NINE

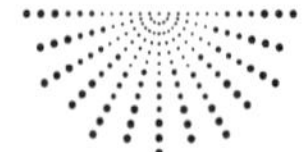

He slammed his hand against the steering wheel. How dare she? His own mother? He drove past the main house and pulled into his sister Katie's driveway. She was Mother's favorite. If anyone knew about what had happened, Katie would.

Short Stuff came out of the house and stared at him. He caught himself before he spoke. He'd better not call her Short Stuff. She had a punishing right hook.

"Katie! You look wonderful!" He smiled as he walked toward her.

"If you were home more than once a century, you'd already know I look wonderful," she scolded. A smile broke across her face, and she gave him a big hug. "I've missed you. How long are you staying?"

He stepped back and followed her into the house. "I'm not sure, yet." He stopped short and glanced around the nearly empty room. "Katie, why didn't you furnish the place? A couch and gigantic flat screen?"

"I have a table to eat at, but as you can see, I have all my computer stuff on it. I don't need things," she explained with a shrug.

"Whatever makes you happy, I guess. Still doing riding lessons?"

She shook her head. "The money is in teaching dressage, barrel racing, and jumping. You know how Montana loves its rodeos."

"Sounds great. I bet it keeps you busy."

She smiled. "All that and competing myself."

"Win anything?" he asked.

"My ribbons and belt buckles have their own room. I'll show you later. Have a seat."

He occupied one side of the couch while she lounged on the other.

"I need to talk to you about Lynne."

Looking away, Katie became engrossed in studying her hands.

"Katie, I know you know. Spit it out," he urged.

Finally, she nodded and looked at him. "Mother never thought Lynne was good enough for you or the McKeegan name. She thought she was after you for your money and the prestige you'd have as a lawyer. She had this crazy idea Lynne was two-timing you. She couldn't see how much in love you two were. Mother vowed to make sure you never married Lynne. I do know she went to Lynne's ranch and told her how she felt. I wasn't mature enough then to tell you. I didn't know anything about heartache."

"So, it's true. I just heard about it today, and I immediately knew she did something to break us up. I should have seen it, but I just didn't want Mother to be the one responsible. My heart feels so heavy. Lynne was never anything but polite to Mother. Lynne told me Mother didn't approve of her, but I told her she must be imagining it." He nervously ran a hand through his hair.

"Why would she do it?" Katie asked softly.

"I told Mother I was going to propose."

"Oh Reilly, I'm so sorry. I know you had a hard time with Lynne leaving." Emotion choked her voice. "I wish there was something I could do."

The silence grew.

"Mother was very convincing about Lynne cheating on you. I never thought to ask who it was or how she knew," Lynne commiserated.

"Lynne is living on our property near the house on the mountain," Reilly disclosed. "Dr. West practically ran her out of town. I came back home to figure a few things out and get my head straight and I found her living there. She hadn't been there long. She was counting on a job in Billings. But West also tanked the job for her." He shook his head, unwilling to get into the details for now. "It's a long story, but she bought a trailer and it's parked near the house. I also gave her permission to use the land up there for her animals."

"Horses?"

Smiling, he nodded. "Among other things. There's a llama, three horses, two opossums, a potbelly pig, and a few others. No one wanted them, so she took them to the barn up there. She didn't ask because Stewart made it known she wasn't welcome on the ranch, but she had nowhere else to go."

"Like an animal rehab?"

"Something like that." He rose. "I need to get going. I appreciate your land use and how you're teaching others."

Katie stood, and he followed her to the door. With an upward reach, she embraced him.

"I forgot just how short you are," he teased.

"I forgot just how overly tall you are." She grinned.

She'd matured over the years, and her plans were sound. He had no doubt she'd do well.

CHAPTER TEN

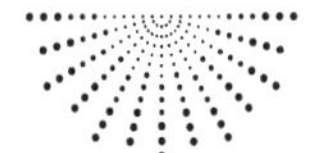

It was pathetic how quickly her things were stowed away. Had she known she wouldn't be allowed back in her grandfather's house after moving out, she would have taken far more with her. A sigh slipped out. Spilled milk.

True to his word, Reilly had hired two men who hooked up temporary water and electrical lines. She hadn't even considered those things, but he was right on the ball, thinking of everything as usual.

Exchanging her boots for work boots, she went to the barn to clean the stalls and cages. This and That had escaped their cages. That wasn't good at all. If their droppings got mixed in with the horse feed, it could be dangerous.

Where could they be? After checking every enclosure, she was stumped. They were probably in the loft. If they contaminated the hay… She couldn't afford to buy much more. So much for budgeting. Of course, the budget was based on her salary at the clinic, so that was a bust anyway.

Climbing the ladder was easy enough. She should have let

them loose a few days ago. Saying goodbye to animals she'd hand-fed since they were young was hard.

The sound of their scampering drew her to the back corner of the loft. They were rolling around. It looked like they were playing. They saw her and stopped. They stared at her and didn't run as she inched closer. In quick order, she had them both in her hands and breathed a sigh of relief. "You two…" she muttered but smiled as they stared up at her.

It wasn't the easiest getting back down, but she managed. Carefully, she put them back in their cage and made sure the door was secure. They'd be let go in a little while.

Quickly, she emptied each stall and scrubbed them down, just in case. Next, she made sure the hay was untouched before tossing some into the stalls. Clean buckets were filled with water.

Ultimately, she found herself coated in fur, feathers, and spit. But one crisis had been avoided.

Now what? She needed to keep busy. It hurt too much to have time to think. So much wasted time. So many lies. His mother had right. Perhaps she hadn't been good enough for the McKeegan name at one point, but she was a well-educated woman now. A doctor of veterinary medicine. Life would have been significantly different if Mrs. McKeegan hadn't interfered.

"You didn't have to dress up for me," Reilly teased.

Whirling around, she put her hand to her chest. "You scared me. I didn't even hear your car."

"Deep in thought?" He nodded as though he knew exactly what she'd been thinking about, and he'd be right.

"This and That got out of their cages. The moment I realized they were gone, the search began. Did you know they could make horses sick? I sanitized everything after I captured my little friends."

"No." He shook his head. "I didn't know. Are you going to put a lock on their cage?"

She shook her head. "No, it's time to let them go. If I keep them much longer, they'll never figure out how to survive in the wild. Can I borrow your car?"

"Of course. I've been meaning to ask you what happened to your car?"

Casually shrugging, her eyes locked with his. "I sold it. Can I have the keys?"

"No." He grinned.

"Because I'm a woman? I remember many comments you used to make about women drivers."

"No." His tone was reasonable, patient. "I'm inviting myself to come along."

He hoisted the cage, and she trailed behind to his car. After he set This and That in the back seat, she slid in beside them.

She tried everything to keep from looking into the rearview mirror and catching his gaze. It was all so painful. Stewart *must* have known. Mrs. McKeegan must have forbidden them from allowing her on the ranch. Made sense. From Reilly's reaction, though, it seemed as though he didn't know anything about it.

Once he had been unable to keep a straight face, especially when he lied, but that was before law school. She remembered him practicing showing no emotion, and he'd gotten good at it.

"How's this place? It's away from any livestock and there's a creek," he said.

"Excellent," she declared, smiling. "This and That, you're going to love it here."

Reilly carried the cage to the creek bank and stepped back.

Before releasing them, Lynne gave each one a cuddle. For a moment, they appeared bewildered, but then they abruptly departed into some nearby bushes.

He smiled. They'd be fine. He turned to Lynne and his breath caught. "Hey, are you all right?"

Lynne's face was streaked with tears. There was only one thing he could do about that. He opened his arms, and she ran to him. He embraced her, drawing her against his chest. This feeling of complete connectedness was one he'd been missing. It surpassed even the victory of an almost impossible case. Somehow, she made him feel exceptional.

She made a hesitant move to back away, but he tightened his arms around her. When she slipped her arms around him, his heart stopped aching.

"Thank you for being here," she whispered. This time, she stepped out of his embrace and he let her go.

"Is it like this with every animal?" he asked.

"No, never at the clinic. But This and That were babies, and I bottle fed them. It was like having twins. I knew not to get attached, but it happened. Mostly I want the animals to be well and able to return to the wild. I'm not sure about rehoming the horses. They would just be an extra mouth to feed. Spitten will eventually go to one of the Llama farms. When Lucky is ready, I'll be proud to return him to the wild."

"You're incredible," he murmured. "Lynne and her menagerie of animals. If you need to add additional buildings or extra fencing, it's fine. I just have to approve them, and of course, Stewart will have a say."

Her radiant smile illuminated her entire face. "Reilly, you have such a kind heart. I'm so lucky to have you as my friend. However, I won't accept anything without offering something in return."

"You're paying rent." He shrugged. "That's enough for

now. We can talk about growth later. How about we go home, get cleaned up, and head out to The Trail Blazer Tavern for dinner?"

She hesitated, her mouth working silently, and he understood she was wary.

"I'll be there with you," he encouraged.

Nodding, she touched his arm. "That sounds nice."

CHAPTER ELEVEN

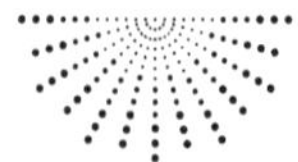

The Tavern's parking lot was almost full.

"I hope we can snag a table," she said, studying the vehicles.

He grinned. "I'm optimistic."

As soon as he was out, he swiftly rounded the hood and opened the car door for her. He had to fight the urge to take her hand. They were friends. He needed to constantly keep that in mind.

As soon as they entered, Dolly Carver smiled at them. She never changed. Always appearing to be in her forties, she emulated her namesake, Dolly Parton, with bleached blond hair.

"Reilly McKeegan, what a sight you are! It's been ages since I last saw you. How goes it?"

"I'm good. I'd ask you that same question, but judging from the crowd, you're doing great. Maybe a table for two, please?"

Dolly shifted her gaze from him to Lynne. "Lynne, nice to see you." Her tone was unconvincing. But she retrieved two menus and guided them to a pleasant table by the dance floor.

"Enjoy your meal!" Dolly said with a playful wink.

Reilly nodded and held the chair out for Lynne. She smiled at him. Once comfortably situated, they both laughed.

"Wow, she's totally into you," she joked. "Was that a wink I saw?"

"It was, yes. However, its meaning was unlike the wink she gave me years ago."

"Bragger."

"It's true. I'm irresistible to women over sixty. It's beyond my control."

In a hushed tone, she said, "We're being stared at."

"Good. A little excitement will do them good." He winked at her, pleased when her cheeks bloomed pink.

"I forbid you from winking at me!" She lowered her gaze to the table, but when she lifted it again, her eyes twinkled. "Plus, I'm immune to your ways."

He chuckled. "My ways? Do tell."

Placing the menu in front of her face, she hid from his view.

"I'm Jennifer, your server. We have a few specials..."

Setting down her menu, Lynne looked startled to see Jennifer.

"I didn't know you worked here, Jennifer," she said.

"Since I wasn't hired by the new clinic, I resigned from my old position."

"I was under the impression the clinic had closed," Lynne commented.

"Just for a few days. It's open until the new clinic is built. The new partner is bringing in his own people, so not all of us will be needed. I left. I wasn't about to be humiliated by continuing to work at a place that didn't want me." Her eyes held a look of sadness.

"I'm so sorry that happened. You have a wonderful way with animals," Lynn told her.

"I appreciate that. It makes a big difference. Now, what would you like to eat?"

Lynne sighed as Jennifer departed after taking their orders. "Jennifer was one of the better ones."

"It's curious to me that the clinic's open while you're without a job."

AFTER TAKING A DEEP BREATH, Lynne forced a smile. "I'd rather not think about that right now. Honestly, I can't recall the last time I dined out."

"You're right. Let's have fun tonight." He stared at her.

"No winking!" she warned.

His response was the slowest, creepiest wink she had ever witnessed. It was impossible to stifle her laughter.

"I agree. We're being watched, probably because they're jealous of you."

"Me?"

"Absolutely, you're with the room's most attractive, brilliant, and humorous man." He smiled as though he was proud of himself.

"Phew, I thought you were going to say in the world. I'll give you humorous."

Many people were dancing together. It had been a long time since she'd last two-stepped. Would he ask her to dance? Perhaps? Perhaps not. Dancing meant being too close to him.

Immediately after they ate, her wish was granted. Reilly put his napkin on the table before he stood. Approaching her, he offered his hand. "Shall we?"

There was no need for words. With her hand in his, the

world felt perfect, if only for a moment. Reilly was a wonderful dancer, and his embrace was comforting. If only... No, she wasn't going there. It invariably led her to regret and anger. There was no need for either of those tonight.

A couple she didn't recognize bumped into them and then asked to exchange partners. Pulling her closer, Reilly shook his head.

"I'm not letting anyone ruin my night," he murmured in her ear.

"My dancing with another man would ruin it?"

He growled softly, his breath warm on her ear. "I also had reservations about his partner. I'm past the age of playing with Barbie dolls."

Laughter once again erupted. "I haven't laughed this much since..." Since him, but she refused to admit it out loud.

He kissed her cheek. "It's been a long day. Ready to go?"

With a nod, she held his hand tightly as he escorted her to the door.

Would he want to kiss her goodnight? It could be nice, but it would lead to trouble. Maybe nice would be very nice and trouble would be far away.

"You look lost in thought," he commented as he parked the car in front of the barn.

"Like you said, it has been a long day. I did, however, enjoy a pleasant evening."

Exiting the car, they found themselves standing before the barn.

"Do you need to check the animals?" he asked.

"I did before we left."

"Oh, well then, goodnight."

Part of her heart betrayed her by sinking.

"I'll walk you to the door," he insisted.

They walked the few yards to her door. "Thanks for the

great evening, Reilly." She turned to walk up the few steps to her trailer. Surprise and relief filled her as he caught her hand and tugged her close. Here it was!

Reilly leaned down and kissed her cheek. "Good night," he said huskily.

She walked into the trailer, turned on a light, and sat down on the couch. She was a fool. Her pounding heart was foolish. Anything they'd once had was a long, long time ago.

CHAPTER TWELVE

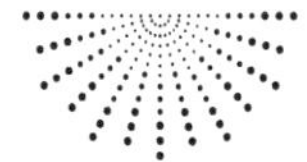

"I've gone over the contracts, West. You owe Lynne a significant amount unless you can produce something to negate this debt. The reasoning behind it all still eludes me." Seated in West's office, Reilly glared at him. "You have told people she killed the McKeegan bull, but that's plain bull. Pun intended. Lynne wasn't on the property the day the bull died. You were. If anyone *killed* that bull, it was you. I have another question about the bull situation. Why didn't you contact the authorities to investigate?"

Calm as West appeared, his stark paleness spoke volumes.

"That would have been McKenna's call. Ask him, he's your brother. Why are you troubling me with this? If you'll excuse me." West stood.

"Sit down. I'm just getting started. You'd be wise to hire a lawyer, as I intend to pursue legal action." He pushed a yellow envelope across the desk. "Here are the preliminary figures for what you owe Lynne for selling the practice out from under her. There will be more as we go over her expenses caused by your sale."

West ignored the envelope, staring at it as though it was a snake.

"That's your copy to go over before our next meeting," said Reilly. "I'll need any paperwork you have regarding that dead bull. Necropsy for cause of death, disposal method and invoice and so on." He stood, adjusted his jacket, collected his briefcase, and promptly exited the clinic without offering a handshake.

Once he stepped outside, Gus waved him over to The Morning Glory Café. Walking quickly across the street, he joined the half owner of the café.

"Good morning, Gus. Nice day."

"Sure is. The sun is shining and we're alive. Had yourself a talk with West, I see. He's a sneaky one. Full of himself, if you ask me. What he did to Lynne was shameful. He drove her out of town. I heard he gave her a bad job reference." Gus shook his head. "How is she? I heard you two were together at the tavern last night." A knowing grin stretched across his face.

Reilly smiled back. Half of his time with Lynne had been spent in the café. "She is just fine and back on her feet. I'm trying to help her with a few legal issues. I thought the clinic closed down."

"Let's get some coffee." Gus opened the door, and instead of ringing, the bell *thunked*, just as it had since Reilly could recall.

They sat at a table, and Ruby Lou hurried over with two cups of coffee. "My, you are handsome in that suit, Reilly. It's great to have you home. How long are you planning to stay?"

"Ruby Lou, are you writing a book about him? He just got here. Let's not frighten him off with any of your plans," Gus admonished.

"Plans?" asked Reilly.

"She's been matchmaking again. Her last attempt had the man stalking the woman."

Ruby Lou gave Gus a withering look.

"If you need anything, let me know." She hurried off.

"A stalker?"

"You can ask your sister-in-law Aurora about that mishap." He shook his head then changed the subject. "So, about the clinic. I was cooking the day West told Lynne the clinic was closed. He told her she was fired. Not two days later, he opened the clinic again. I didn't know how to get a hold of Lynne. As far as I'm concerned, West is a crook! Lynne is such a nice girl. You know you could do worse. You were always a happy couple."

"I can hear you, Gus! Sounds like matchmaking to me!" Ruby Lou gave him a frosty look before she turned her back on him.

Both men held in their laughter.

"I'm Lynne's lawyer," Reilly told Gus in a low voice, "and if you hear anything, please call me. This situation is sketchy, and it's difficult to find the starting point."

"Take care, Reilly," Gus said as both men stood.

"Come again soon and bring that pretty gal named Lynne with you!" Ruby Lou called out as he opened the door.

"Spike, you should have seen This and That. They were as happy as can be. She ran a hand down his leg; the joint looked good. "I'm going to let you out in the pasture tomorrow."

She stood up and stretched her back just as the potbellied pig snorted. "Tuni, I hear you. I'll be there in a minute."

If not for her animals, she'd go crazy. She'd had a restless night and slept fitfully. It was overwhelming trying to consider everything. Getting a trailer for herself had been a wise move, though. Now she had a place to live without crowding Reilly.

"Here Tuni, come eat." The miniature horse snuffled her arm. "Yes, Mini, it's your turn. But first you need brushing."

All night long, she berated herself for longing for his kiss. He claimed not to have sent his mother, yet she had seemingly been privy to their plans to marry in a year. She'd known quite a bit about their plans, actually.

Wiping her hands on her jeans, she remembered how his mother had told her she wasn't fit for the McKeegan name. It was quite possible that realization would have hit her before they married. Especially since the thought of living close to Mrs. McKeegan had often given her pause. Reilly had always appeared to remain unaware of the continuous barbs and the contemptuous glances she received from his mother.

Her grandfather had been so welcoming toward Reilly. Maybe things had worked out for the best after all. Her life would have been lived in constant discomfort in his mother's shadow.

Her musing drifted toward the accusations David West had made about a McKeegan bull. There had to be a way to clear her name.

"Mini, I need to locate where they disposed of the bull. I can't just sit here knowing West has my clinic open. That man stole from me." Maybe Reilly could help her figure things out. Mini shook her head as Lynne pulled the brush along her shoulder. "No, I am not the type of woman who needs saving by a man." The horse snorted. "You're right, Mini, I need to go to town. I have no reason to hide."

After she cleaned herself up, she picked up her helmet and put it on. Where to start? It didn't matter; she just needed to get into town. Mounting her bike, she started it then sped down the driveway and headed toward town. The bank made the most sense. West remained uncooperative; however, the bank was obligated to explain to her West's acquisition of her family ranch.

Her anger was far beyond simply hot under the collar. She drove through town and parked in front of the bank. Tyrone Savings and Loan. The appropriate name would be Tyrone, the Stealers of Property. She took a few breaths and waited until she was calm. She'd play dumb and ask for a copy of the paperwork. Perhaps a smile would do the trick—if she could muster one.

She opened the door and went inside, her heart pounding with apprehension. With its shiny marble floors and long velvet drapes, the building was truly beautiful. And intimidating.

Tellers conducted their business from mahogany workstations consistent with the rest of the wood. Who had built this? It was strangely posh and ornate for such a small town.

"How can I help you?" a thin, tall man inquired.

"I need a copy of a loan taken on a mortgage. It's for the Walsh property. The IRS wants to be sure they got their money." She smiled, pleased with her clever reasoning.

"I'm not sure if that can be handled here."

"Miss Walsh, it's wonderful seeing you again," Carl Rodgers, the bank president, boomed as he approached.

"Yes, well, I need copies some papers of my grandfather's."

"Please come to my office." He entered a door off to the side, and she trailed behind.

With a gesture, he indicated she should sit, which she did.

"Now, what is this about your grandfather?"

"I need access to the mortgage on the property, the loan taken out and any payments made. The IRS is claiming I made money on the sale of the property, but from what I remember, my grandfather never paid the loan in full. The bank took the property."

Frowning, Carl rested his elbows on his massive desk. He bent forward. "We're sorry, but we dispose of papers after a certain number of years."

She leaned forward. "Legally, you must keep them on the property for seven years. I'm sure you could print out the documents for me. We aren't in the 90s anymore. Banks are progressive. They must be to meet government regulations."

"It'll take some time to research and find the information you're looking for." Leaning back, he smiled.

"Maybe if we were talking about many years past, but my grandfather died three years ago. I'm not sure what the issue is." Darn, she'd forgotten to play stupid. "I'll wait while you get that information printed. Or…my lawyer can visit you, if you prefer."

"From where does this attorney hail? There are no representatives from Tyrone acting on your behalf. I would have known."

"Why is that?" She stared at him.

"Why is what?"

He was stalling. "Expect a visit from Reilly McKeegan. However, he'll probably need more information than I do."

Carl laughed. "Honey, that ship sailed long ago. Don't expect assistance from the McKeegans; Reilly wouldn't represent someone as insignificant as you. You're really a nobody. He has a large practice based in Billings."

"Yes, he does." She stood and continued to stare at him. "Good day, Carl." Head held high, she left. It might be a beautiful building, but something sure did stink in it.

CHAPTER THIRTEEN

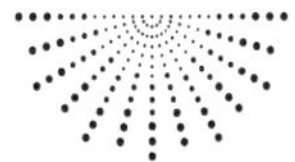

The roar of a motorcycle reached Reilly from outside. Good, Lynne was home. They had a lot to talk about. Nothing personal, though, just business. He had come very close to humiliating himself last night, when he'd been tempted, too tempted, to kiss her.

Business, just business.

Only after she entered her place did he leave the big house. It wasn't necessary for her to be aware that he'd been observing her. He ambled to the trailer and knocked.

"Hey, come on in. I was just coming to see you." The room brightened with her smile. "Sit, the couch is comfy."

He sat down. Why did she want to see him?

"My recent meeting with Carl Rodgers was very insightful, I believe."

"The banker?"

"Yes! He's hiding something. I wanted the papers for the mortgage and loan on my grandfather's property. According to him, they have a brief record retention policy. I told him he had to have them for at least seven years for the IRS."

“He didn’t give them to you, did he?”

She sighed loudly. “No, he said they can’t be found easily on the computer because it was so long ago. When I said I’d have my lawyer collect the documents, he practically laughed in my face. He informed me that he would know if I had a lawyer. When I said your name, his smile was sickeningly wide. He said you were too busy and successful to represent someone insignificant like me. A nobody.”

She sank back into the chair as though she’d just finished a marathon.

A scowl pulled at Reilly’s brow. “He had the audacity to call you a nobody? I could never stand that pompous idiot. Are you suspecting West's actions were a land grab after your grandfather's death?”

“Something along those lines,” she muttered. “There is so much that doesn’t make sense. I’m upset with myself for letting that happen. I reacted to their actions by withdrawing. I should have asked more questions. I regret not standing up for myself and demanding answers. I’m so stupid.”

“First of all, you are not stupid. Secondly, you defended yourself today. It seems you managed old Carl perfectly.” Reilly smiled. “In the meantime, I met with David West this morning. He’s an overblown liar. He didn’t say anything, but I informed him I was your lawyer and put him on notice I was looking into the clinic as far as your contract is concerned.”

Her eyes widened. “What was his reaction?”

“He turned a bit gray.” His lips ticked up as he recalled the satisfaction of seeing West squirm. “It’s important to stay vigilant about our surroundings. I have a hunch that this involves more than just West and the bank. Did he mention to you about having a new partner?”

"Yes, and they were expanding on a big piece of land. You heard Jennifer last night. West isn't keeping everyone on. The people I worked with were always top-notch. I never had a problem. I could probably pick up all the employees he's letting go and set up my own clinic, but there would be no way to compete against the clinic he's building." She deflated a bit.

Business, just business. But he desperately wanted to hug her.

"Could I possibly have a personality defect?" she questioned softly.

He hesitated. Was this one of those traps that, no matter what he said, he'd be wrong? "I'm not sure what you mean."

"Do I tolerate others walking all over me without complaint? Your mother told me you sent her to end our relationship, and I never reached out. West welcomed my investment, but later modified the terms verbably, a change I accepted without comment. They kicked me off the farm, and I never protested. Clearly, I'm a weak and easily manipulated person."

"I wouldn't say that," he mused softly. "Why would you even think you were being lied to? You've lived in this town all your life. You know all the people involved. The truth is harder and harder to find these days. I recall a time when honesty was common. Although not always the case, you'd expect those you grew up with to be honest. It's starting to seem like a chaotic jumble to me. For example, is false news actually false? Who decides what is fake? So, what exactly is misinformation? The word misinformation means lie. Newspapers and TV news were once considered reliable sources of truth. The news is now biased, only presenting stories that support a certain agenda. It may be a political issue, or money could be the deciding factor. Speaking one's truth often leads to censorship." He drew a deep breath then slowly released it. "Once I enjoyed debating ideas, but challenging the dominant narrative is now labeled as 'misinformation.' Things are not always as they seem, I've come to believe. We need to ask questions." He shook his head. "Sorry for the long speech."

"No, don't be sorry. You're savvier than me. And yes, I agree; I never would have guessed West would attempt a deception. My education is costly, but I'm learning. Do you mind me telling Carl that you are representing me?"

He smiled. "No, not at all. I am representing you."

LYNNE NODDED. If only she was in a position to tell him she didn't need him.

"I appreciate it, Reilly. But you don't need to remain in town for my sake." He didn't deny he sent his mother. He'd had the perfect chance, and he'd let it slide by. All that talk about truth was irrelevant if he was lying. His actions seemed to make any relationship impossible. The words his mother spouted that day still haunted her.

She stood. "I'm going to work with the animals and then enjoy a quiet night."

"I have some work to do, too. Enjoy the rest of your day." And with that, he left.

What was West up to? Why was he helping her? And why wasn't he telling her *how* he was helping? He should have told her directly that his plans did not involve her. Her grandfather's loan wasn't a secret.

And then it hit her like lightning on a clear day. For an educated woman, she was incredibly stupid. No eviction papers existed. As the estate's executor, she had been informed that all assets had been transferred to the bank.

Grief had taken over. But where had her common sense been?

She stared out the window without seeing anything. She'd spiraled after the loss of Grandpa. What were the stages of grief? Maybe she'd gone through all of them at the same time? It probably didn't work that way.

She grabbed her Stetson and headed out for the barn. She had animals that needed her. Trusting her instincts about animals had never let her down.

Later that evening, a knock at her door gave her a fright. Upon opening it, she encountered West's angry stare, and her heart rate ramped up. Why hadn't she used the peephole? He pushed his way past her.

"West, it's so lovely to see you," she said, dripping with sarcasm.

"I'd like to talk to you." His authoritative tone made her want to laugh.

"About what?"

"In reference to you sending your lawyer after me. I'm surprised you aren't shacking up with him."

She flicked her outside light a few times as she closed the door.

"So, what was it you wanted to say? You're probably here to offer an apology, right?" She smiled brightly.

"Why apologize? You only have yourself to blame. I had nothing to do—"

The door swung open, revealing Reilly. "Am I late to the party? Doesn't matter, I suppose. I have a game we can play. Who here is full of the most nonsense?" His grin was incredible.

"I'm not sure, Reilly," she started. "Why bother playing a game we're both going to lose? What's the fun in that?"

Reilly winked at her, and she started laughing. He had to put a stop to his winking.

West' eyes glinted. "Reilly, have you told Lynne the truth about why you're in Tyrone? We're all puzzled as to why you abandoned such a stunning wealthy woman."

Only Reilly's foot-shifting betrayed his discomfort. Lynne forced herself to keep an even expression. She hadn't known about a woman in his life. The impact was worse than a slap to the face.

"Reilly doesn't keep secrets from me. West, you should go." She walked to the door and opened it. She stared at West, who shrugged and then glared at her as he left. The lock on the door engaging was loud in the silent room.

"I'm grateful for your help. I didn't know what to do, and I hoped the lights would catch your attention. I suppose I should make you number one on my phone. I also should have looked to see who it was before opening the door. You did say to be on the alert." She plopped down on the couch, leaning her head back. "I have no preservation instincts, it seems."

Reilly sat down in a chair across from her. He didn't say a word.

Was he still involved with this woman? His mother probably approved of her.

"If I wasn't staying at your house, would you have made an effort to see me?" Anticipating a harsh response, she held her breath.

"I hadn't planned on seeing anyone. I just needed some time alone." He stared just to the right of her.

"I apologize for any inconvenience I've caused you." She released a heavy sigh. "My problems are mine. Don't make them yours. I'll be fine. I won't be here long. My inability to secure a job means I cannot afford my rent. Perhaps a smaller town...or a bigger one, or maybe even moving out of state. I have a lot to think about. Preparations I should have completed." She offered him a shaky smile. "I'm so tired. Do you mind?"

Sorrow and pity were both evident in Reilly's eyes. It was as if a spike had pierced her heart.

"Of course," he murmured. "But I wasn't planning to leave anytime soon. My plans are not definite. I'll keep you updated on my progress. Good night."

CHAPTER FOURTEEN

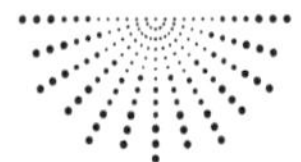

The door opened, then closed. Getting up, she locked it again. After making herself a cup of tea, she sat back on the couch. There had to be a logical way to figure out what had happened.

Number one, her career. She had been in the top five percent of her graduating class.

Number two, A prominent vet, David West, had extended an invitation for her to join his practice. Wait, she was being too generous in her assessment of him. The county had only had one vet, and it was him. So he had been prominent only by virtue of the fact that he had no competition. Even so, she'd felt it was an honor to be asked.

Number three, she'd gotten the money to buy in to the clinic from her grandfather, who had claimed it was money sitting in the bank. There was something amiss about that. Why borrow against his house when he had money in the bank? Had he instead given her money from a loan he'd obtained? But even if he had, she had been helping with loan payments. Thus, it logically followed that the loan was used to purchase half of the veterinary practice for West, paid for by Lynne and her grandfather.

In any case, when her grandfather had become ill, there had been no financial reserves to help with medical needs. But it mattered that David West had benefited from her grandpa's generosity.

After Grandpa's passing, the loan repayment was never questioned. The option of selling property to settle the loan hadn't been raised with her. The sale of the property should have at least given her some money. Why had she been so naïve?

Heck, with numbering her problems. Stewart's refusal of access to his property was also a key factor. It became common knowledge around Tyrone that she was incompetent. Though she lived in a small town where gossip spread quickly, she was innocent. Yet no one had questioned Stewart's decision to exclude her. West was rarely around, so she ran the clinic. He took all the house calls. When they did interact, he'd made comments suggesting she limit herself to cats and dogs. He'd also checked the daily patient list, and his remarks had implied that certain pet owners would not let her near their animals.

Groaning loudly, she punched the couch cushion. She had played the perfect victim to whatever West had been planning, most likely the new clinic. But he'd also said she wasn't up to par for the McKeegans.

With a shaky breath, she inhaled and then slowly exhaled. Many times, she had wept alone, believing herself a failure, that she was disliked and didn't fit in with others. It had been done over two years, and she had obviously been too stupid to put the pieces together. Well, to be exact, her problem wasn't stupidity, but gullibility.

It wasn't so surprising that she'd formed her own band of merry animals. They'd become her family. And now, she could only hope that Reilly could get her some type of settlement so she could relocate her trailer and her animals. A clean slate, someplace where her heart would be safe.

REILLY WAITED in the bank parking lot, anticipating its opening. He had some unfinished business with Carl Rodgers. A grin tugged at his lips. He excelled at this. Or at least he'd used to. His plan was to inspect the property once he had the paperwork. A visit to David West would cap off his day, should he have the time. He was certain to have an interesting day.

Finally, the bank security guard unlocked the door. Whistling a happy tune, Reilly leisurely got out of the car and walked into the bank. He didn't say a word, just went to Carl's office door and opened it.

"McKeegan, you're not allowed in here. I'm about to join an online meeting."

"There's still time to send your apologies for not attending." His grin returned. "We have a lot to discuss. We'll begin by addressing how you acted toward Miss Walsh yesterday." With a tilt of his head, he squashed the grin and scrutinized the banker. "Is the board cognizant of your habit of belittling customers? Your behavior was highly unprofessional. Not only were you rude, but you also refused to help Miss Walsh. Well, I'm Miss Walsh's representative, and I prepared Mr. Walsh's will. That was among my initial tasks as a lawyer. A good man, Mr. Walsh. And now, I require all documentation pertaining to the Walsh accounts, loans, mortgages, and the property sale. I'd like to see payment history. In addition, I need copies of all checks issued in the last ten years."

"Some of that will need time, um, to be addressed. I told Lynne—"

"Miss Walsh to you."

A bright red flush seeped into Carl's face. "I explained to Miss Walsh that not all the papers were present. She understood."

"You're now up against me, Miss Walsh's lawyer," Reilly reminded him. "Most of the data is saved on the computer and easily accessible. Are you familiar with how to use one?"

It looked like Carl Rodgers' face was on fire. "Each check, transaction, loan, and mortgage inquiry will incur a fee." A glint shone in the man's eyes.

"Mr. Rodgers, do you recognize me? I imagine landing the McKeegan ranch as a client is quite substantial."

"Stewart's in charge of the finances," Rodgers maintained through clenched teeth.

Reilly got his phone and hit a button. After one ring, his brother answered. He set his cell phone on speaker.

"Hey, Stewart." Reilly kept his gaze on Rodgers. "I'm at the bank, and Mr. Rodgers is giving me a hard time. What other bank should we move our business to?"

"I prefer local banks, but I'm open to switching. I can arrange the transfer—" Stewart said.

"Wait! There is no need. Mr. McKeegan, I will gladly provide you with your information by the end of the day."

"Thanks, Stewart." Reilly pressed end.

Standing, Reilly fastened his suit jacket. "I will see you before you close." He picked up his briefcase and walked out of the office without closing the door behind him. He briefly nodded to the gawkers before departing.

How uplifting this investigation felt in contrast to his last case. He was giving help to someone who truly deserved it.

David West was out of his office all day, and no one at the clinic seemed to know where he was. Reilly shrugged. He'd catch up to the vet, eventually. He wouldn't be able to hide indefinitely.

His next stop was the community center, where he hoped he could ask Joanne Sumpter to collect the bank papers for him.

"Is the world coming to an end? You're here!" Joanne exclaimed, rising from the reception desk to embrace him.

"Good to see you too, Jo."

She took a step back. "I go by Joanne now. It's more professional, or so I was told."

"Let me guess that old wind bag Ethel Homes made you change it?"

Joanne made her way behind the counter. "Something like that." She smiled.

"No ring on your finger?" he asked.

"Just like you," she said. "Remember when we were kids? We said we'd never get married. And here we are. What can I do for you? Incidentally, I like your suit."

He grinned. "I was hoping you could do me a favor. I asked Mr. Rodgers to pull information for me, and I told him I needed it today. The bank is open for seven more hours, and I really don't want to wait around."

She answered with a chuckle. "Yes, I'll get the information from Mr. Grumpy."

He laughed, and it felt liberating. "Thank you. I'll let him know to expect you and I'll stop by in the morning to pick it up."

"Go on, enjoy your day. Honestly, it's so good to see you, Reilly."

"You too."

He climbed into his car and made a call to the bank. Rodgers was not available, a secretary told him, so he left a message to expect Joanne Sumpter to collect the information he'd requested.

He and Jo had been the best of friends during their childhood. Jo was such a tomboy and so much fun. The trouble they used to get in had probably given both sets of parents gray hairs.

Those memories stayed with him on his drive home.

He emerged from his car to find Lynne speaking with the wolf. What was its name? Lefty? He walked to the barn.

"How's Lefty?"

Her lips twitched. "*Lucky* is ready to be released. I need to call Montana Fish and Wildlife Commission first. They'll probably want to take care of it themselves."

"Lucky sure is lucky he found you." A lighthearted feeling settled over him. "I went to the bank. Carl promised all the information and paperwork by end of day." He grimaced. "I'd forgotten how pompous he can be. I had to go so far as to call Stewart and ask him to change banks. Stewart went along and Carl caved. Unfortunately, West wasn't at the clinic and no one knew where he was since he's almost never there. He's got them all trained to lie for him. That's probably why your friend from the tavern wasn't offered a job at the new clinic."

"You can check again after you go to the bank." Lynne had moved on from Lucky and was doing something to the hawk. Left Wing?

"How's the bird doing? Left Wing?" he asked.

A smile lifted her lips. "*One Wing* is improving rapidly. He probably wants to go where his name is known."

He chuckled. "Well, I remember people's names. And I know a few of the animals. There are Paint and Bay. Piggly Wiggly and—"

A tinkling giggle burst from her lips. "You're full of laughs today. Her name is Tuni. The other horse, who isn't named after its color, is Spike. Of course, the horse you are standing in front of is Mini."

"Wait, I do know the llama's name Spitten." His pride at recalling the llama's name is inexplicable to him.

"I recognize that smile. It's the Reilly well done smile."

"I ran into Joanne Sumpter today. She's going to pick up the papers from the bank for me. She looks the same."

"Still beautiful. I remember when you gave a kid at school a black eye for calling her your girlfriend." Lynne laughed.

"Jo was never called my girlfriend after that." His grin grew wider remembering those times.

His phone vibrated. After answering it, he had the response he'd wanted.

"We have permission to inspect your grandfather's property."

CHAPTER FIFTEEN

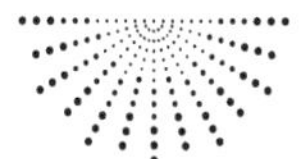

We have permission to inspect your grandfather's property. Remembering the words as Reilly drove them along the highway to her old home jolted her. Some days it was hard enough to drive by her used-to-be home. So much had happened in the last few years. It was as though she had gradually become invisible to everyone around her. All that she cherished had been lost.

But she refused to go down that road filled with pain. Stepping onto the ancestral land, knowing her failure to protect it, was already going to be incredibly difficult.

How did one just summon strength? Was she too sensitive to be cold and unfeeling? It was just land, after all. If she had to go, though, Reilly would be the person she'd have picked to go with her. He looked at things in such a way that most things were either right or wrong. Though he saw the shades of gray and took them into consideration before making a judgment.

Turning his head, he offered a smile. "We're almost there. You okay?"

She nodded, not trusting her voice. Her throat

constricted when the ranch came into sight. The fate of their small number of animals remained unknown to her. Buckle, her grandpa's dog, had died the same day.

After the car stopped, she beat Reilly to opening the door, exiting the car before he could help. Bulldozers had destroyed the barn and half the house. Wooden stakes with flags of various colors littered the property. Even the large oak tree with her tire swing had disappeared.

The area appeared deserted. It might be after quitting time.

Taking a deep breath, she let it out as she took a step toward what used to be her house. She clapped a hand to her chest. They hadn't bothered to empty it. What a mess. The porch and front two rooms were gone, leaving the rest wide open. All the things she hadn't been allowed to take with her mocked her.

"They left half the house."

"Maybe they realized the value of the antiques in it."

"Antiques? We used all of those to pay for his treatment. Most of what was left was a bit old, but not that old."

Reilly remained silent as he studied their surroundings.

"Do you think it's structurally sound to go inside?" she asked. Not waiting for an answer, she walked to the family room and kitchen and hopped up into them. Everything remained exactly as she had left it. She lovingly ran her hand along the oak dining table.

In the kitchen, she opened a cabinet and fished out a tin can. Opening it, she laughed at the wad of bills inside. "I can't believe I'd forgotten about this. At least they didn't get all of his money. He never did trust Mr. Rodgers. Said the man left a bad taste in his mouth."

"That sounds like him," Reilly said with a chuckle.

"Reilly, is it possible to halt this so I can retrieve my things? I'd like a few mementos of my family. Look, the family Bible is still there. I'm taking it today." She picked it up and clutched it to her chest. "I got the raw end of the deal, didn't I?"

"Excuse me a moment." Reilly walked away, dialing his phone. Happiness shone in his eyes when he came back.

"I called the judge. The demolition shows their disregard for anything of value here. Everything's yours; there's a two-day injunction on the demolition."

Her jaw dropped momentarily. She unexpectedly embraced Reilly. That hug was a total expression of thankfulness. The hug she received in return was a balm to her soul.

"Let's get movers scheduled. Oh my, who can we get on such short notice?" There also was no money to pay for movers. "I think I'll just take what I can put in your car. Maybe if we make a couple of trips?"

"That's my Lynne, too proud to ask for help." He smiled gently. "I've already made the necessary arrangements. They'll come tomorrow. Let's fill the car today; afterward, we'll arrange for someone to bring the horse trailer."

"I can't let you do all that—"

"I want to do it for you." He looked deep into her eyes. What was he trying to convey? Was he trying to make up for sending his mother to cut her into pieces?

Swallowing hard, she nodded. "Okay." She'd accept his gift, but no matter how many gifts he gave her, she could never truly, honestly love him until he apologized. Maybe not even then.

"Too bad we don't have boxes," he commented.

Laughing, she pointed to a cabinet door. He opened it, and his eyes widened.

"Grandpa saved every plastic bag he ever received. You never know when they'll come in handy, he'd say."

"Strange as it is, they'll help today. But I do think boxes

will be in order. Would you mind if I quickly go into town to pick some up?"

"I'm a grown woman, Reilly."

He started to wink.

"Don't you dare! See ya!" She laughed.

As soon as he left, she went straight to her grandpa's bedroom.

Standing in the doorway, a wave of despair tore through her. Her cheerleader in life was gone. He'd always been so sure that anything she did was the right thing. He had never allowed her to doubt herself. Second guessing wasn't acceptable.

The watch he always wore still sat on the bedside table. It wasn't an expensive watch, but it had been his father's and he'd worn it with pride. He'd said it reminded him that you didn't have to have the most expensive or the newest. Reliable things in life sustained him.

Antiques? Smiling, she shook her head. He would have had a good laugh at that. Carefully, she gathered the photos he'd framed and put them into a bag along with a sweater he often wore. It still smelled like him. The last thing she added to the bag was the crucifix that hung on the wall.

As she turned to leave, the floorboard creaked, and she laughed. The hiding place. There was never much in there, but why not check? Kneeling, she pried up the floorboard, revealing a metal box.

Puzzled, she lifted it up, placed it on the floor and opened it. Inside was a silver necklace her mother had once worn. What a treasure! There was also the deed to the property. She tucked both items into another bag and put it inside the first one that she had almost filled.

She heard the car and stood, but before she could go to the front to greet Reilly, she was blocked by West. He stood in the hallway, looking beyond mad.

"I just got the call. All of this belongs to me now. You have no right to be here. It's called trespassing. I suggest you leave as soon as possible. Though I didn't see your bike outside," he said in a condescending tone.

"No, no bike today." She pushed past him to the kitchen.

"You're lucky I edged you out of our practice instead of allowing you to be sued. I did you a favor, and you call Reilly to help you? He laughed when you finally went back to school. I believe his exact words were 'good riddance.'" He stepped closer. His face had turned an angry shade of red. "I want you gone. Gone from this house and gone from Tyrone. I can deal with the McKeegans. Who do you think they'll believe? You?" he mocked.

"I wish I could say you don't scare me. Did you wait until I was alone?" She nodded at his flinch. "That's what I thought. I no longer care what other people say or who wants me gone. I don't require your approval to live my life." She quickly took her bag and hopped down to the ground. Walking away wasn't being afraid, it was being smart.

She had her mementoes; she didn't need more. Her memories would sustain her. It wasn't worth the fight. She'd just keep looking for the opportunity to live and work where she'd be happy.

Was that Reilly's car? Hard to tell, but then she realized it was coming from the wrong direction.

CHAPTER SIXTEEN

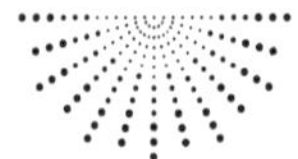

His heart raced until he finally caught sight of her on the side of the road. To all appearances, she was fine. Pulling over, Reilly got out of the car.

"Flashlights would have been a good idea," she said wearily.

"Taking you with me would have been a better choice." His attempt at a smile resulted in a wince.

Lynne quickly moved to stand before him. "Reilly, what happened? Is that a black eye?"

"Yes, I'm fine. Nothing a little ice won't fix. Let's get in the car." He held the door open for her, attempting to evade her gaze.

After getting in, he started the car. "I had a little run in with West back at the house. He sucker punched me. Who does that anymore? He acted like he was a teenager. Back then, I didn't have much use for him either."

"He told me to leave. He wasn't pleasant about it, but he didn't touch me."

Reilly studied her face and then nodded. She was fine. He could finally breathe.

"Let him be. I don't need things. What would I do with all that furniture, anyway? You were being kind, calling it all antiques. I believe the correct term is junk. I have a few things, and I don't need more. I don't want anything else to happen to you." She turned and looked out the window.

"He has no right to it."

She nodded. "I know. I found the deed to the property. I need to see the loan papers. I'll let the law deal with him; I'm not going to confront him directly. If he stole the ranch..."

"We can take a look at the papers when we get home. I stopped by Jo's place and got them." he murmured. What was running through her head?

He parked in front of the house and they went inside. She was unusually quiet.

"Are you sure West didn't hurt you? Have a seat. I'll make tea." He waited for an answer, but she didn't say a word. Glancing over his shoulder, he noted that she was engrossed in reading the information from the bank.

Lynne smiled her thanks when he set her cup in front of her. "Do you know who Prime Horizon Holdings is?"

He froze then swallowed hard. "It's my mother's. I don't think she uses that holding company anymore. Why?"

"She owns the property." Lynne threw the papers down and walked out of the house.

Shocked, Reilly looked at what Lynne had been reading. His heart sank. There it was, his mother's holding company on the deed. He'd have to go through all the statements to see when she bought the ranch. As soon as he had all the facts, he needed to have a talk with his mother.

It didn't promise to be a pleasant talk.

SHE WAS the fool once more. She was baffled by Reilly's ability to keep a straight face while interacting with her. It was likely Stewart was also laughing at her.

It had already been an emotionally charged day, what with seeing her old house and now this. This was worse than being sucker punched. It was like being run over by a semi. Just how many times was she supposed to pick herself up and dust herself off?

After she entered her trailer, she sat in the dark. Her head pounded. Her hard head, obviously. There was no use asking why anymore. What right did his mother have to interfere in her life once again? If she could easily pick up and leave, she would be on her way out of town.

Funny, though, how West claimed the property to be his. Not that it mattered anymore. What was the point of living in a town where she was constantly getting kicked in the shins? Enough was enough.

She started searching on her phone for jobs. She should never have left it at home. She'd need to make improvements to her resume. Her laptop had long since given out, but she could probably afford a tablet. Prices weren't so bad. Tomorrow she'd see which one came with what and order one.

Now, to find an article on how to make a resume shine without a referral.

UPON REVIEWING EVERYTHING, he wished he'd never begun. A couple of things were clear. His mother had written Mr. Walsh a check for one hundred thousand dollars around the time Lynne had left him. Was the check in payment for Lynne staying away from him?

His stomach lurched. Lynne probably didn't know. The

ranch was at that time free and clear of all debt. The mortgage was paid off. Then a year later, his mother filed a lien on the property and Lynne's grandpa began to write checks to the holding company.

That paperwork was missing. The checks provided no information regarding what they were for. He'd have to find the lien papers. He needed to visit the courthouse to inquire about it.

Mr. Walsh had then taken out a loan from the bank, probably to pay Reilly's mother, but it looked as though she had never removed the lien.

That must be why the ranch didn't go to Lynne. Why hadn't she been notified?

That was as far as the paper trail went except for a large check written to David West. He felt as if his eyes would start bleeding if he looked through any more of the paperwork Rodgers had gathered. He needed answers before he had a talk with Lynne. It appeared she had more than one good reason to hate his mother.

She was probably upset. He wanted to comfort her, but without the answers, he didn't know what to say to her. The lights were out at her place. Odd, because she always slept with one light on. It had been the light above her stove, but…

Had his love for her triggered all these events? Had her life been ruined by their relationship? His mother had been quite brilliant. She'd ensured he would never ask about Lynne.

What would their lives be like if she hadn't interfered? Would they have had kids by now? There was really no sense wondering *what if,* but he couldn't help the thoughts. His mother, predictably, wouldn't shoulder any responsibility. She'd most likely say she'd done him a tremendous favor.

Not good enough for his family. There wasn't much of a higher society in Tyrone. There were a few of the rich who kept to themselves, but there wasn't a country club or many social gatherings where only the wealthy could attend.

None of that had mattered to him. It still didn't. Nothing irritated him more than the people in Billings who wanted to know him just because of his last name. That was precisely why he didn't date.

el at his feet. "I'm sorry, I can see I caused

have nothing to apologize for. I've known
nd you've always been a fine man. Is Reilly

heard a bunch of yellin' before I left." A
lled up the drive. "Oh good, there are the
rse trailer. You know, it didn't sit right with
animals in the trailer. I planned to let them
went down. Fish and Wildlife took the wolf
hough. I had to call them. They said they'd
n and make sure the wolf was fit and hawk
efore they let them go."
k you. Did any of my animals give you a

kled as he burst out in laughter. "Only that
That is some gross stuff. Had to put a clean

s put the trailer back and hooked up all the
she lovingly took each animal out, gave them
efore she put them where they belonged. She
imal for signs of cruelty, but she found none.
with tears, which she furiously dashed away.

G A FIT. It was as though through her squeals
the story of what had happened. After eating,
then, the men had left.
with her feelings was a bit much. She needed
Sable's extreme measures to force her out of
hate wasn't a sufficient reason.
now she looked at it, she couldn't remember
been rude to Mrs. McKeegan. Mr. McKeegan
n kind to her, but that was long ago. Reilly's

CHAPTER SEVENTEEN

Lynne studied the empty space where she had been living over the last few days.

There was nothing left. The trailer was gone and, more importantly, her animals had been removed. She'd only been away for a few hours. Well, maybe a bit longer. It turned out to be a wasted effort; the reported injured horse wasn't real.

Horrified, she stared. She walked through the barn to see if maybe Lucky and One Wing were left behind. Few people would deal with a wild animal. The food was still in the barn. No, the only reason to leave food behind was because they weren't going to be fed.

Rushing from the barn, she vomited violently. With tears in her eyes, she wiped her mouth. Then she pulled out her cell and called Reilly.

He didn't seem to believe her at first, but the panic in her voice likely convinced him that the situation was serious. He was heading home.

Home, a word that could mean nothing special or it could mean everything. He'd wanted her gone, but this was more than just cruel; it was inhumane. Her heart broke. Where were her animals? Maybe she should have called the sheriff. If only Reilly would hurry.

Sitting on the top step of Reilly's porch, she rocked herself back and forth. It became hard to breathe.

Lord, please protect my animals. I'm scared, Lord. I know You are always watching over me, but I'm too rattled to think clearly. My only comfort is You.

Relief coursed through her at the sight of Reilly. He was barely out of the car before she ran to him and wrapped her arms around him, holding on to her only friend.

"You weren't kidding." He shook his head, contrition on his face. "I'm sorry, I know you weren't kidding, but to see it. Oh, wow. I'll call the sheriff. Did you ever call Fish and Wildlife?"

"No, I planned to do it today. They wouldn't have taken the trailer."

His phone rang. What was that ring tone? It grated on her.

"It's my mother," he said before he stepped away to take the call.

"I absolutely refuse to let her speak to you. Return all of it. You're out of line. No, Stewart didn't command it. I'm coming right over."

"Your mother did this?" Deflated, she sat back down on the steps. "Why?" Abruptly, she was overcome with a rage she'd never experienced.

Once again, Sable McKeegan had reduced her to a frightened young girl.

Reilly kissed her before leaving, but it hardly registered. What gave this woman the right to interfere where she wasn't wanted? *Am I so objectionable?*

Lynne went into the barn and cleaned out all the stalls and cages. Next, she replaced the water with fresh water and mother had always acted like she was better than others. She was like the queen bee, determining who was in and who was out. Most people in Tyrone just put up with her. She didn't go into town too often.

REILLY WALKED into his brother's office. He gave Stewart a nod before looking at his mother. She smiled as though she was glad to see him. She smiled as if she hadn't done one thing wrong. She smiled as though all was right with the world.

It left him seething.

"Mother," Reilly said before he took a seat.

"Reilly, dear, no hug for your mother?"

He glared.

She shrugged and turned her attention to Stewart.

"I want to turn the pastures up there into training grounds. Katie is teaching rodeo riders these days, and she needs a bigger barn and better horses. The barn that's there can be knocked down. It's of no use to us."

Don't lose control. She's trying to get to me.

Stewart scowled. "We built a state-of-the-art barn and indoor arena for Katie. She designed and oversaw everything about it. The outdoor arena has been regraded to be perfectly flat. I went with her to an auction to buy four new horses. Have you *talked* with Katie?"

"Stewart, your idea of state-of-the art is archaic." Their mother waved her hands, a ring with a large red ruby flashing in the light. "I know what went on around here and how you were conned out of our fortune. What topped it all off was your marriage to that woman. For heaven's sake, her father is the one who made a fool of you. What is wrong with you?"

"Now, wait a minute," Reilly interjected. "I didn't come here to talk about Stewart. Building on my land is out of the question. How are you justified in taking Lynne's trailer and animals?" Though outwardly calm, his rage was about to erupt.

"Reilly, you can't imagine my distress when I heard about that awful Walsh girl living on my property, next to the house you chose. I couldn't catch my breath for a long time. What in the world do you think you are doing?" Her slick smile and condescending tone wore on his last nerve. "She made a life of her own without you. Why are you back at the ranch? Go back to Billings and live the good life. Search for a suitable woman to date."

"A suitable woman. It all comes down to me finding a rich wife from an impeccable wealthy family, doesn't it?" He huffed in disgust. "You probably have a few choices you consider suitable for me, right? Mother, I'm a grown man, a lawyer. I am not a child to be manipulated or given ultimatums." Despite his desire to remain calm, his voice grew louder.

"I didn't give you an ultimatum. You should get your facts straight, counselor. I do have a say as to what the land on this ranch is used for. Especially our section. No trailer or the trash that comes with it." She angled her head and smiled again.

"Because it's not a permanent structure, the trailer is not subject to your approval," he ground out. "She is paying rent."

"Oh? I wonder how an unemployed woman can afford rent," she sneered.

Stewart stood. "Mother, you are out of line. I mean, so out of line. Lynne pays me money to stay on that piece of property. I okayed it. Like Reilly said, it is not a permanent structure."

CHAPTER SEVENTEEN

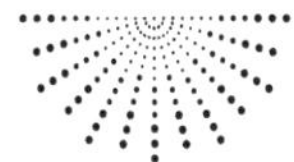

Lynne studied the empty space where she had been living over the last few days.

There was nothing left. The trailer was gone and, more importantly, her animals had been removed. She'd only been away for a few hours. Well, maybe a bit longer. It turned out to be a wasted effort; the reported injured horse wasn't real.

Horrified, she stared. She walked through the barn to see if maybe Lucky and One Wing were left behind. Few people would deal with a wild animal. The food was still in the barn. No, the only reason to leave food behind was because they weren't going to be fed.

Rushing from the barn, she vomited violently. With tears in her eyes, she wiped her mouth. Then she pulled out her cell and called Reilly.

He didn't seem to believe her at first, but the panic in her voice likely convinced him that the situation was serious. He was heading home.

Home, a word that could mean nothing special or it could mean everything. He'd wanted her gone, but this was more than just cruel; it was inhumane. Her heart broke. Where were her animals? Maybe she should have called the sheriff. If only Reilly would hurry.

Sitting on the top step of Reilly's porch, she rocked herself back and forth. It became hard to breathe.

Lord, please protect my animals. I'm scared, Lord. I know You are always watching over me, but I'm too rattled to think clearly. My only comfort is You.

Relief coursed through her at the sight of Reilly. He was barely out of the car before she ran to him and wrapped her arms around him, holding on to her only friend.

"You weren't kidding." He shook his head, contrition on his face. "I'm sorry, I know you weren't kidding, but to see it. Oh, wow. I'll call the sheriff. Did you ever call Fish and Wildlife?"

"No, I planned to do it today. They wouldn't have taken the trailer."

His phone rang. What was that ring tone? It grated on her.

"It's my mother," he said before he stepped away to take the call.

"I absolutely refuse to let her speak to you. Return all of it. You're out of line. No, Stewart didn't command it. I'm coming right over."

"Your mother did this?" Deflated, she sat back down on the steps. "Why?" Abruptly, she was overcome with a rage she'd never experienced.

Once again, Sable McKeegan had reduced her to a frightened young girl.

Reilly kissed her before leaving, but it hardly registered. What gave this woman the right to interfere where she wasn't wanted? *Am I so objectionable?*

Lynne went into the barn and cleaned out all the stalls and cages. Next, she replaced the water with fresh water and put hay in the stalls, hoping beyond hope, her menagerie would return.

Could she press charges? After all, Sable had stolen her animals and her home. She sighed. That would never happen. This moved up her timeline to find a place to live and secure employment. Anything that came close to what she needed would work. The ability to be selective was gone. Sitting on the steps, she took her phone out of her pocket. She'd continue with the want ads and then branch out.

Next, she went to a site for professionals and scanned the jobs for veterinarians. Two sounded promising, though one was out of state. That meant getting a license to work in that state.

It was down to one, and she'd do it without telling a soul. That was the only way to have a true fresh start. Although Reilly only desired friendship, the prospect of leaving him caused her pain.

The money she'd taken from the tin at her grandpa's house ended up being a hefty sum. Why he didn't use it to secure his ranch, she'd never know. Her world was now a confusing and disordered place.

A truck hauling her trailer came up the drive. Why did she have to be here to witness them *un-stealing* her home? It was ridiculous and embarrassing. It was probably all-around town that Sable tried to kick her off the ranch.

The driver of the truck was Bernie, a ranch hand who had been with the McKeegans for what seemed forever. She remembered him from when she and Reilly had been dating. He got out and gave her a sheepish grin.

"A few of the boys are coming to put it back. I honestly didn't know you didn't ask for it to be moved."

"Where was it?"

"Parked as close to the road as I could get. When Mrs. McKeegan asks you to do something, you do it." He kicked at a cluster of gravel at his feet. "I'm sorry, I can see I caused your distress."

"Bernie, you have nothing to apologize for. I've known you for years, and you've always been a fine man. Is Reilly coming too?"

"Eventually. I heard a bunch of yellin' before I left." A pickup truck rolled up the drive. "Oh good, there are the boys and the horse trailer. You know, it didn't sit right with me to leave them animals in the trailer. I planned to let them go after the sun went down. Fish and Wildlife took the wolf and the hawk, though. I had to call them. They said they'd take care of them and make sure the wolf was fit and hawk was able to fly before they let them go."

"Bernie, thank you. Did any of my animals give you a hard time?"

His eyes crinkled as he burst out in laughter. "Only that spitting llama. That is some gross stuff. Had to put a clean shirt on."

The cowboys put the trailer back and hooked up all the amenities while she lovingly took each animal out, gave them a bit of loving before she put them where they belonged. She checked each animal for signs of cruelty, but she found none. Her eyes welled with tears, which she furiously dashed away.

TUNI WAS HAVING A FIT. It was as though through her squeals she was telling the story of what had happened. After eating, she calmed. By then, the men had left.

Being alone with her feelings was a bit much. She needed to understand Sable's extreme measures to force her out of town. It seemed hate wasn't a sufficient reason.

No matter how she looked at it, she couldn't remember one time she'd been rude to Mrs. McKeegan. Mr. McKeegan had always been kind to her, but that was long ago. Reilly's mother had always acted like she was better than others. She was like the queen bee, determining who was in and who was out. Most people in Tyrone just put up with her. She didn't go into town too often.

Reilly walked into his brother's office. He gave Stewart a nod before looking at his mother. She smiled as though she was glad to see him. She smiled as if she hadn't done one thing wrong. She smiled as though all was right with the world.

It left him seething.

"Mother," Reilly said before he took a seat.

"Reilly, dear, no hug for your mother?"

He glared.

She shrugged and turned her attention to Stewart.

"I want to turn the pastures up there into training grounds. Katie is teaching rodeo riders these days, and she needs a bigger barn and better horses. The barn that's there can be knocked down. It's of no use to us."

Don't lose control. She's trying to get to me.

Stewart scowled. "We built a state-of-the-art barn and indoor arena for Katie. She designed and oversaw everything about it. The outdoor arena has been regraded to be perfectly flat. I went with her to an auction to buy four new horses. Have you *talked* with Katie?"

"Stewart, your idea of state-of-the art is archaic." Their mother waved her hands, a ring with a large red ruby flashing in the light. "I know what went on around here and how you were conned out of our fortune. What topped it all off was your marriage to that woman. For heaven's sake, her father is the one who made a fool of you. What is wrong with you?"

"Now, wait a minute," Reilly interjected. "I didn't come here to talk about Stewart. Building on my land is out of the question. How are you justified in taking Lynne's trailer and animals?" Though outwardly calm, his rage was about to erupt.

"Reilly, you can't imagine my distress when I heard about that awful Walsh girl living on my property, next to the house you chose. I couldn't catch my breath for a long time. What in the world do you think you are doing?" Her slick smile and condescending tone wore on his last nerve. "She made a life of her own without you. Why are you back at the ranch? Go back to Billings and live the good life. Search for a suitable woman to date."

"A suitable woman. It all comes down to me finding a rich wife from an impeccable wealthy family, doesn't it?" He huffed in disgust. "You probably have a few choices you consider suitable for me, right? Mother, I'm a grown man, a lawyer. I am not a child to be manipulated or given ultimatums." Despite his desire to remain calm, his voice grew louder.

"I didn't give you an ultimatum. You should get your facts straight, counselor. I do have a say as to what the land on this ranch is used for. Especially our section. No trailer or the trash that comes with it." She angled her head and smiled again.

"Because it's not a permanent structure, the trailer is not subject to your approval," he ground out. "She is paying rent."

"Oh? I wonder how an unemployed woman can afford rent," she sneered.

Stewart stood. "Mother, you are out of line. I mean, so out of line. Lynne pays me money to stay on that piece of property. I okayed it. Like Reilly said, it is not a permanent structure."

"Fine," she snapped. "The trailer can stay, but not that woman. She must leave!"

Reilly rose and faced his mother. "She stays, and I don't want you on my portion of the property. Mother, I'm warning you to stay away from Lynne. She has been through enough."

"Yes she has. No job, no ranch, no prospects." She released a gusty sigh. "You reap what you sow."

He left before he did something he'd regret. When he got into the car, he took several deep breaths and smacked the steering wheel. He took a moment to calm down before driving home. When had she become so cold, so calculating? He still had papers he was waiting on about the sale of the Walsh ranch. And he had a feeling he wouldn't like what they would reveal.

The biggest question was why did his mother hate the Walshes?

CHAPTER EIGHTEEN

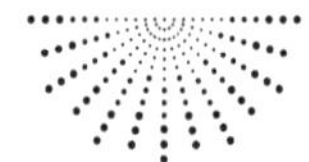

Shortly after the men setting up her trailer left, Reilly arrived. He smiled as he exited the car, but it wasn't a happy smile.

"How'd it go? Do I have to leave?" Lynne held her breath.

"No, you're staying."

"Did you see your mother?"

Reilly stiffened. "Unfortunately, I did. I'm trying to think back. I never remember her being devious or so cold. Come on inside. We have a lot to talk about."

Nodding, she followed him into his house. Her body was rigid with fear. Reilly had a frightening and unreadable look on his face.

He motioned for her to take a seat at the table then began to make tea. Only when tea was served and Reilly sat did the silence in the room break.

"It was my mother who had your trailer and animals taken away."

"I know. I just don't know why."

Reilly sighed. "Initially, she stated that all buildings

required her approval. Not true, by the way, plus the trailer isn't a permanent structure. She claimed that she needed the land to build a top-of-the-line barn and arena so that Katie could train her students. Stewart blew that out of the water. Katie had a whole new setup built earlier this year. Apparently, Mother hadn't been contacting Katie as frequently as I believed." He settled his gaze on Lynne. "Is there any reason you can think of why my mother might have a problem with you?"

She shook her head. "I have been going over every encounter with your mother, and surprisingly, there weren't many. I know for a fact I was always respectful toward her. I felt her cold disdain the first time I came here with you, as your girlfriend. I never went inside your house when we were kids. Your father was always happy to see me, not that I was here often."

"Now that I think about it, Jo was always allowed in the house. But she never visited as a girlfriend." He shook his head. "I strongly suspect it involves your family. I'm still figuring things out; these papers are a puzzle, and I haven't found all the pieces yet."

"A puzzle? Your mother never approved of me. My Grandpa once voiced his surprise that our relationship was allowed when we first started dating. I never asked what he meant. I figured it was because I'm poor. I was then and I still am. I'm not sure I want to know the reason." She lowered her gaze to her hands, clasped in her lap "I think I have a lead on a job. It would be best for me to move and start over in a community where I can avoid the whispers."

"Lynne..." he murmured.

"It was harder than I can describe to go to work each day after your brother refused to speak with me about one of his horses. The clinic staff gave me a wide berth. I'd walk into a room, and it was suddenly quiet and they all looked guilty. I was dropped from all invite lists. Grandpa would tell me to hold my head up high. Then he passed away, and I was abruptly evicted, only being allowed to take my clothes and phone. Of course, I forgot the charger. When I moved into Gus' place, I got looks of pity from the whole town. I can't figure out why West betrayed me. I regret not moving sooner, while I still had use of my truck. But there were the animals that no one else would help." A tear trailed down her face. Why was she rambling on so? She needed to just shut up.

Reilly handed her a tissue. "I'm so sorry. Here is what I have learned so far. Around the time we broke up, my mother wrote a check to your grandpa for one hundred thousand dollars. Yes, he cashed it. His mortgage was paid off by a transfer from his account. Then, for some reason, a lien was filed against the property by Prime Horizon Holdings. My mother owns that company. Then your grandpa wrote monthly checks to Prime Horizon Holdings. That went on for a year. The checks stopped when your grandpa secured a loan for twenty-five thousand dollars. One half of that money went to my mother and the other half went to West as your buy into his practice, but the lien was never removed. There were a few checks written for your college, but the amounts were never huge. I had a time puzzling that out. I know you got a scholarship plus financial aid."

"Yes, the checks were for what he called 'walking around money.'"

"You mentioned you'd been paying on the loan for your grandpa."

"Yes, I made a big dent in that loan. I made weekly payments. Between Grandpa and me we had just written our last check. The loan was paid."

"Right now, the problem is there is no record of you paying off the loan."

Panic set in. A shiver ran down her spine as her hands shook.

Reilly scooped her up and put her on his lap. His embrace always felt special, but her body took a long time to recover.

"I'm fine. You can let go of me."

Reluctantly, he placed her back on her feet and then went back to his chair. Her distress was painful to witness, especially as it stemmed from his mother.

"I intend to show the loan was settled, thus ending my mother's right to a lien on the property. I will also determine how my mother transferred the property to West. It's a convoluted mess."

She sighed but said nothing.

"How did the animals fare?" he asked, changing the subject.

"Fine. Fishing and Wildlife took Lucky and One Wing. I have faith in them. I've worked with them before. I don't want to spring anything on you, so I might as well tell you." Lynne stood and went to the window, her back to him. "There is no place for me in Tyrone. It's been a long time coming. Intentional actions were taken to destroy my reputation and steal everything precious to me. I can't fight back. The damage has been done. Working as a vet around here won't be possible for me again. I'm like the animals I've collected, deemed not worthy to keep."

"Lynne—"

"Please don't interrupt me. I'm so happy we reconnected; you're a wonderful and respectable man, and I'm proud to have you as a friend. The things your mother said to me that day. She highlighted my shortcomings, giving reasons why she believes I'm not good enough. She informed me as well that you had a significant other at school. Cruelty was in every word she said."

"I'm—"

"I need to get this all out. I'm not looking for sympathy; I just want to explain what had occurred. Her words damaged my confidence and they still do. Back in school, I found her assessment accurate: I was utterly lacking. In hindsight, I should have known we'd end. The loneliness was almost unbearable. I only came home for a week in the summers. I didn't leave the ranch; the ringing house phone constantly panicked me.

"Once a car pulled into our drive, and I hid in the barn until my grandpa found me. He calmed me and got me to promise I'd return home following graduation. I saw in his face how selfish I'd been and how much he depended on me. Truthfully, it was a relief you never came home for holidays. Working as a vet helped to grow my confidence. I felt less lonely; I was beginning to find my place. Well, you know the rest."

She turned and her eyes glistened. "I'll leave as soon as I can. I need to live and work somewhere I'm appreciated. I'm finished with the ranch and my partnership with West. I have to leave this behind."

The lump in his throat refused to go away. Listening to her shattered his heart. She deserved a place where she could make friends. He'd make it happen for her.

"I'm so sorry, and truly I understand your need to get away from this place. I'll support any decision you make." He hesitated. "But Lynne…there was never another girlfriend waiting for me at school. I only wanted you." His voice was raspy. "I wish I had known my mother came to see you. But we can't change the past. What's done is done. You are a beautiful, competent woman and you deserve to live the life you want." He couldn't take his eyes off her. She was lovely, even in despair.

She nodded and then stood and left. A piece of him went with her.

CHAPTER NINETEEN

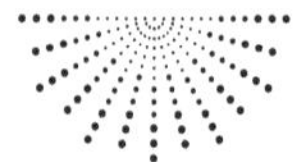

Lynne waited for the crew assigned to transport her trailer and animals. She worked closely with the Fish and Wildlife Conservation to obtain and file the necessary paperwork. There was a barn on the property she'd found, and a small house that needed a ton of work before she could move in. It was cheap. To her astonishment, the local vet gave her a temporary position after their meeting until she could set up her own clinic. The combination of her salary and the conservatory grant would allow her to manage financially.

She'd spent the last week cleaning and sanitizing the barn. The stalls were ready for her friends. A few fenced-in pastures provided grazing areas for the animals. The trailer had electricity, but the house alone had plumbing. It didn't make sense to go to the expense to have water in her trailer.

Reilly had gone over every contract before she signed them. Leaving him was going to be difficult. In the six weeks since her revelation, they had become closer. They deepened their friendship while respecting each other's need for space. It was such a relief and surprise to know he didn't send his mother to break up with her. It made a huge difference, yet it wasn't the difference she'd imagined. Their lives were different now. Reilly was going back to Billings. And she would have no reason to come back to Tyrone.

He said he'd call often, but she was skeptical. They'd probably talk every few days, then only once a week until they someday only spoke on the holidays. Her heart never stopped hurting. Her love for him might fade someday.

The honking of a truck had her running out of the barn. Everything was ready to go. The horse trailer was filled. The plan was to follow the trucks on her motorcycle. A mix of relief and sorrow washed over her as she donned her helmet.

Reilly drove up next to her. She had hoped to avoid saying goodbye.

"I'm glad I caught you," he said. His smile was strained and unconvincing.

She removed her helmet. "Me too. I can't stay long. I'm following the trucks to my new home. I've dreaded this moment. I wish I could say we'd get together soon, but it wouldn't be true."

He nodded. "I'm going to miss you. I'm even going to miss your menagerie of animals. Take care of yourself and don't hesitate to call if you need anything."

Tears filled her eyes. "I'm just going to say see ya." She stepped close to him and he wrapped his arms around her. He kissed her neck and then her cheek before letting go.

"See ya," he whispered.

His heart cried out for her, but there was not one thing he could do to change their circumstances. Proclaiming his love for her wouldn't have been fair. She had a chance to do what she always wanted, and he loved her too much to stand in her way.

He stood there long after she left. He was completely lost and didn't know what to do. He planned to go back to Billings, but frankly, he had no desire to do so. Stewart's suggestion was to work the ranch. Get back on a horse.

In truth, his relatives had given him a cold reception when he began his legal studies. Perhaps Stewart was right; maybe working the ranch would be a positive change.

The empty space where the trailer had been hit him hard. Rubbing the back of his neck, he went inside where he wouldn't have to look at it.

The next day he found his cowboy clothes at Stewart's. Not everything fit. When he'd left, he'd been a boy, but now he was too broad-shouldered to fit into the shirts.

"You're trying to get out of riding. You probably forgot how," Stewart teased.

"Can I borrow some of your clothes? I'll get my own after work. The Daily Provisions still sells clothing, doesn't it?"

"Yes, it does. Take anything you want from my closet. I'm looking for bulls online. There's an auction coming up, and I'd like to replace Thor."

"Having all the information in front of you must make it easier than it used to be," Reilly commented.

Stewart smiled. "Still the same lies that were in the brochures. The pictures help, though I've found them to be wrong too."

"Thanks for the clothes." Reilly took what apparel he needed, reminded that he still had to look into Thor's death.

"Well, you're a sight for sore eyes," Bernie, the longtime cowhand, said.

"It's been a while. How's it going?"

"It's going. I don't ride as much as I used to. My knee acts up at times."

"You hurt your knee rodeoing, didn't you?" Reilly asked.

"Yes, when I won the all around in 1988. Don't think I'm shirking."

Reilly laughed. "Never. You'd do all the work yourself if we let you."

He saddled up his horse, Law, and rode toward the cowboys in the distance. They were separating the females from the males. What type of greeting would he receive? He wasn't in the mood.

His cousin Cassidy rode out to meet him. He was smiling, a good sign.

"Good to see you. You've been missed. Come on, let's see if you can still, cowboy."

Reilly laughed and followed Cassidy to the herd. It took a few minutes, but soon enough he was riding as though he had never left. The camaraderie was a balm to him. There was something about the great outdoors, with the mountains and blue sky, that had a positive aspect.

It was a long day in the saddle, chasing cattle that refused to cooperate. He even had to rope a few, and his rope skills were still good.

It wasn't until he got off Law that he felt it. His muscles protesting his action with pain. He should have eased into it, but like everything else in his life, he'd jumped in with both feet.

Stewart came out and handed him a tube of Bengay. "You might need this," he joked.

"Oh, boy, I'm going to smell like an old man. Well, if it helps, it helps." He winced as he walked toward his car. "I'll grab my clothes and bring these back in a few days."

"You mean you won't be here tomorrow?"

"Stewart, you were always a brat." He smiled and then groaned as he eased himself into his car.

CHAPTER TWENTY

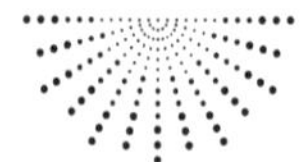

It was everything she'd dreamed of and more. The small town of Potter had been more than welcoming. It had everything a person could need, plus it wasn't too far from Great Falls. They were the kindest people she had ever met.

They were thrilled that they would finally have a veterinarian of their own. A minimum two-hour wait for a vet's response had been typical before she came.

Judging by the number of pies received, it seemed every woman in town was a pie maker. She received an invitation to their Tuesday morning coffee. They all met to catch up weekly. There were two diners in town, so they alternated.

Troy Waddy was the local house builder/carpenter. He generously offered to fix her house since it was slow at the office. Though she suspected he worked from his home. She'd heard a baby cry the last time she talked to him on the phone.

He was such a cheerful person, and a dose of positivity was just what she needed. Plus, he liked to take home pies.

When she explained she couldn't afford to pay him yet, he

smiled. "I know you will when you can." It almost brought tears to her eyes.

She found a place in town that would serve as a clinic. All she needed was a little elbow grease.

Everything in Potter was different. She received her loan for the clinic right away. All the supplies she needed would be within her reach. Shopping online was her greatest pleasure. There was room to expand the building eventually.

For the moment, she made house calls. A lot of house calls. It seemed those folks she hadn't met through pie-giving had an animal that had a small ailment. It gave her a sense of being needed, unlike ever before.

Quickly, many mothers were trying to set her up with their sons. While it was nice to know she was good enough, she declined all their invitations. Keeping busy helped in the broken heart aspect. It was when she was alone at night, that she'd think only of Reilly. She imagined him going to parties with clients. That would be expected. A piece of her wished for his joy, while another yearned for his love. Honestly, her longing for him was substantial.

She prayed each night, thanking God for her many blessings, and she always asked that Reilly would find happiness. He deserved that much.

CERTIFIABLE. That was what his family had called him when he moved to Great Falls and set up his practice. He wasn't interested in a high-profile legal career any longer. He excelled as a lawyer, yet he disliked public attention.

He looked around his new apartment. It was spacious, with an outstanding view, but maybe it was too big. He'd taken a page out of his sister Katie's book and didn't buy any furniture that wasn't absolutely needed. It wasn't as though he'd be entertaining.

His practice had grown in the last two months and he finally hired Kelly Stock. She was fresh out of college and eager to learn. The demand for new clients and high billable hours was a thing of the past. He could do what he wanted. The core of the problem was his inability to find something he wanted.

He went to a few meet and greet type events. It was different from past ones he'd attended. Business wasn't all that was discussed. No one was trying to be the peacock of the room. It was quite pleasant.

His ability to be himself, in contrast to his inability to do so in Billings, was striking. Enlightening too.

He no longer talked to his mother but had been back to the ranch to spend a weekend here and there. The sight of couples walking sometimes made him feel cheated. It was worse when they had a young child. He and Lynne had never called each other, as promised. He waited and waited, but she just…never called.

But he had business to discuss with her, and he couldn't put it off any longer. He also had a check for her that she probably needed. He'd finally received each piece of paper he needed to put the puzzle together. She needed to know.

His call to her ended with an awkward silence that left him feeling sad. He still had to handle the business related to her property and her stake in the clinic. She invited him to come to her new place.

Of course, he knew where it was since he'd set it up for her. But she didn't know that. Today he'd see her. Excitement and dread warred within him. He was at his limit with heartache. Packing up his briefcase, he took a deep breath and started his trip to Potter.

He'd be at her place any minute. Maybe she should have just had him send everything in the mail. It would have been preferable to pacing and peeking from her trailer window.

It was a bit of a drive from Billings. He'd probably go to the ranch after their meeting. She was excited to show him her place. Showing him her clinic would be fun. She still needed a few things and hoped to find them at a nearby auction. She already hired a med tech, Noreen Flannagan. She was reliable, and she was great with animals and their owners, too. Scott Richards had come highly recommended. Next would be a receptionist.

Would he be happy for her? No, no more doubting or relying on anyone's approval to feel good.

The sound of gravel crunching reached her ears. There was his car. She stepped back just far enough so she could observe him without him knowing. He was so handsome; he always had been. The confidence he exuded was fascinating. She had to look away before she decided she loved him.

The smile in his eyes when she opened the door warmed her heart. No one ever looked at her the way he did.

"Come in! It's good to see you."

"It's good to see you, too." He stepped forward as though he was going to hug her, but he stopped just short of doing it. "This looks to be a great piece of property."

"Thanks, have a seat. I made coffee for you and tea for me."

He smiled as he sat down at the table. Then he opened his briefcase and pulled out a few thick folders.

She put their drinks on the table. "Those files look huge."

"We have a lot to go through." He opened the first folder. "The first order of business is the dead bull. There *was* no dead bull. David West and my brother McKenna sold the bull and claimed it died. I hunted down Thor and had a DNA test done. Their greed knew no bounds. But that's one mystery solved."

A flash of rage gave way to relief after a deep breath, but she remained somewhat upset. "Why blame it on me?"

"They got a lot of money and discredited you. I bet they thought themselves clever." He sighed. "Let me start at the beginning. Your grandpa wouldn't allow your father to marry Sable. He thought her to be crass, and he also thought she didn't really love your father, she just loved how much the ranch was worth."

She stared at him, speechless.

A wry smile lifted his lips. "I was surprised too. That's why she never gave you a chance and got you out of my life. Because we had nannies, I didn't realize how unkind she was. She wasn't around much. Our father raised us. I never imagined she'd say you weren't good enough, and that I was seeing someone else. She bribed your grandfather to silence him and keep you from me. Your Grandpa used the money to secure your future. He paid off the mortgage on the ranch. He paid West to buy in to his practice on your behalf. My hunch is that your grandpa didn't want you to know how he got that money. Then my mother decided to ruin your grandpa and filed a lien on his ranch. With the help of our preferred banker, she prepared the loan documents and requested payment. Your grandpa got a loan from the same bank and paid her off. She never removed the lien.

"Your grandpa was left to pay the bank loan. He paid, you paid, but those payments were never recorded, and the money is missing. I have a good idea who took it."

It felt as though all the blood drained from her face. Lightheadedness engulfed her. How could this be true?

He leaned forward, peering at her. "Are you feeling all right? Your face is so white. I apologize for rushing; I should have given you more time to absorb what I was saying." He stood and got her a bottle of water from a case on her counter. "Drink this."

Nodding, she drank some of it. Sable McKeegan was the puppet master, and she was the unknowing puppet. How far had her reach extended? Were the grades she thought she earned in college real? In a flash, she was up and running toward the bathroom. Without closing the door, she leaned over the toilet and got sick.

That woman had ruined Grandpa's life and hers. Her grandpa took money from that witch to keep her away from Reilly? Quickly, she brushed her teeth and went back to the table.

"This affected your life too."

"Yes, in a way I can't forgive."

CHAPTER TWENTY-ONE

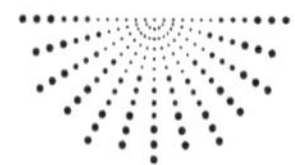

Reaching across the table, he covered her small hand with his. Hers was cold as ice.

"I've had a while to figure this all out. It's been shocking and hurtful, to say the least."

"Yes. I suppose West and your mother hatched a plan to run me out of town." Her smile was brittle.

"Yes. Stewart didn't know that by refusing to speak with you about his horses, he was doing you harm. He really thought you had played me for a fool." He paused a moment to study her. She was still pale, but she no longer looked as though she would collapse. "Now, West does not own your property. You do. He has no legal right to your property and the lien against the property has been declared void. In fact, West owes you a lot of money as per your contract with him. Here is the check for what West owes you.

"Carl Rodgers was fired, and charges are pending. You will eventually receive all the money back that was paid on that loan. West has been served papers to appear in court next week. The deed to the property is in your name. The best part is he's in jail at the moment for his part in stealing Thor." Reilly sat back in the chair. "I think that's all of it."

"Oh, how evil it all was! Convoluted too. I'll never forgive your mother. In many ways, she broke me."

Sorrow settled in his bones. "She's not in my life anymore. She let me think you left me without a word. She observed my suffering, but it didn't affect her. I understand she caused you pain, and I'm truly sorry. She went to great lengths, and I think she enjoyed it. To her, it was a chess game. That was completely and terribly wrong."

Lynn nodded. "I'm sorry she hurt you. That is not how most mothers act. You deserved her love, not her devious games to control your life. Well, now, we know the truth."

An awkward silence filled the air as he stared into her eyes. What was she thinking? The silence was agonizing. It appeared she was bidding farewell. Her sorrow ripped his heart apart. They couldn't go back, and it didn't seem as though she wanted to go forward.

He put the files back in his briefcase, all except for the deed and the check. Standing up, he gave her a sad smile and started for the door. The pain in his heart was more intense than ever.

"I-I was going to show you around. I'm having the house fixed up, and the barn is in good enough shape for now. I have a clinic in town that I plan to open soon. I'm working with another vet, older guy, making house calls at the moment." She sighed. "You probably want to get on the road. You had a long drive from Billings."

"I don't live in Billings. I moved to a town more laid back than Billings. I can be myself there and not some *Wonder Lawyer* to be put on display. My number is still the same if you need anything."

He left before she could reply. He was incapable of making conversation. For some reason, he pictured her understanding their injustice and wanting to restore their relationship. Dreams were for suckers.

SHE SAT, not moving, trying not to think. Tears poured down her face. "Oh, Grandpa, I wish you had sold the ranch before taking money from Sable McKeegan. Taking money to keep me away from Reilly? How could you? You saw how destroyed I was after her chat with me." Lynne slapped her hand down on the table.

That woman infected and destroyed people and their lives. It felt like Sable had fractured her once more. When Reilly left, he seemed more than just upset. She'd tried to get him to stay longer, but he'd seemed determined to leave. He hadn't seemed at all interested in how she had picked up the pieces of her life.

The reality was that she and Reilly had embarked on new lives. The best course of action for them was to move on.

How her heart disagreed with her head. Her heart was inconsolable. It wanted a different outcome.

She began to repay their conversation. How much did David West owe her? Picking up the check. She was astounded by the amount it was written for. Should she sell the ranch? She would be able to afford a new barn, pay Troy and much more.

The phone rang. It was Troy. He wouldn't be by in the afternoon. The baby had been up all night and his wife needed to sleep.

A sigh slipped free A baby…

REILLY COULDN'T HELP HIMSELF. He parked in front of the building Lynne planned to use for the clinic. It looked to be in good condition. Her life was filled with wonderful events that were moving her forward.

The town was small, like Tyrone, quaint with all the small stores. There were two diners, and it looked one restaurant. He could imagine the owners of the diners competing for customers. At the end of the street, he saw a church with a steeple. It had been a while, but maybe it would soothe his heart.

Walking down the sidewalk, he could feel the friendliness of the people he passed. A nod, a smile, a "good morning." After all Lynne had been through, she would thrive in this community.

A plethora of stained-glass windows enhanced the beauty of the church. He sat on a pew, stared at the crucifix for a moment before he kneeled.

Good morning, Lord, I hope You have a moment for one of Your flock who has strayed. Not strayed and doing things I shouldn't, but strayed because I haven't been to church in a few years. My life has been turned upside down. Secrets, vendettas, greed and lies are the reason, but You already know that. The whole thing has yanked my heart out, but I learned a few things too. I can be myself and people like me. If things don't seem right or add up, there is some digging to do to get to the truth. The next one is hard. I need to forgive my mother somehow. I'll need Your help. I also need to find a way to let Lynne Walsh go. She's finally happy and I can't take the chance of ruining it for her. Lord, I give You thanks and praise.

A few moments later, he left. It was time to make a fresh start of his own. Except for testifying against the people who tried to steal from Lynne, he had no need to see her again. It's unlikely those cases would go to trial. Before getting into his car, he looked at the clinic. "Good luck, my love," he whispered.

CHAPTER TWENTY-TWO

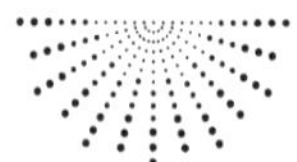

Aside from the occasional document and check through the mail, four months had passed since her last contact with Reilly.

Life was hectic, but she liked being busy. She hired Scott Richards to work as a vet tech. Thankfully, he and Noreen worked well together. Tina Flatt became her receptionist. Tina knew everything about everyone. Tina could prove to be a minus instead of a plus.

Troy had worked wonders, and her house was ready to move in. She didn't feel as excited as she'd anticipated. Same as opening the clinic, a huge milestone for her, but it lacked something. They held an open house at the clinic, and the attendance pleased her. Not one person whispered about her.

She was making friends, but something held her back from making close friends. Was it a trust thing? Hopefully, it was an *it will take time* thing. Of course, she had her menagerie of animals. Bay was ready to give birth and with her having twins, it was nerve-wracking. She prayed all three would live.

A couple of months ago, she'd hired a man named John

Black. He was a bit slow, and no one else would hire him. Most people had run out of patience with him. But he was a nice man who was twenty years old. His enthusiasm always made her smile. He took care of her animals. It didn't matter how long it took for him to clean stalls and feed the animals. The horses, Spike, Bay, and Paint doted on him. She swore Bay batted her eyelashes at him. Tuni and Mini took to him right away. Spitten took a while, but he slowly warmed to John.

Even the new additions liked John better than her. Feathers the ostrich and Hippity the rabbit.

He had a real knack with animals.

Reaching Mr. Clay's ranch, she stopped her car. His horse had gotten loose, ran into the woods and cut her neck. Lynne got out of her truck, grabbed her bag, and walked to the barn. The sound of the horse shrieking hastened her steps.

"Oh my, she's in pain." Lynne opened the stall and slowly went in. Mr. Clay held a towel to the horse's neck.

"It's mighty deep, Lynne."

"Let me give her something for the pain so I can examine her." The whole time she worked to calm the mare, Mr. Clay hovered over her. It wasn't the biggest of stalls.

"Mr. Clay, can I have you step out of the stall? I'm going to need more room."

He did as she requested. After washing off a lot of the blood, she shook her head. "She's been shot."

"What?" Shock laced his voice. "I didn't see a bullet hole."

"It grazed her. She was lucky, but you'll want to call Montana Fish and Wildlife to report it."

"Will Butterball be okay?"

"I'm just going to stitch her up and put a bandage on her. It won't take long."

While she stitched Butterball up, she smiled. She had to

call him Mr. Clay, yet he didn't call her Dr. Walsh. He wasn't much older than she was. People and their quirks.

She finished with Butterball, showed Mr. Clay how to put on the bandage in case it came off.

"I'll be here tomorrow."

Her phone rang. When she answered, John sounded upset. "The twins!"

"I'm on my way!" She called Scott on her way home. She'd need his strength.

Scarcely had she switched off the car when she rushed into the barn. Bay was certainly starting to give birth.

"You did great, John! Go into the trailer and grab the towels I left on the table. All of them." She touched the mare on her neck. "It's going to be fine, Bay. I can't wait to see you with your two babies."

John was back in a flash. "I've got the towels."

"Put them next to me. Now, I need you to get one of the new buckets and fill it with fresh water and bring it here."

By the time John finished, Bay had delivered one of the foals. It was tiny and it lay in the straw without yet trying to stand, but its breathing was good.

"Bay, I'm going to have to shift the other one," she murmured. "Everything is going to be fine."

Her phone rang. "John, could you take the phone and answer it for me? Tell whoever's calling that Bay is having her twins."

John took the phone and stepped out of the barn. "Yes, Doc Lynne is having twins. It's a hard birth and the second baby isn't out yet. Yes, I'm sure." John ended the call and left the phone outside.

Reilly frowned. Was he mistaken in what he heard? Lynne was having twins? He called back three times, but it went to voice mail. Swallowing hard, he tried to remember if Lynne had looked pregnant the last time he had seen her. He hadn't spent much time with her. He saw her four months ago. Twins were tricky, they came early, didn't they?

He frowned. And just who was the father?

He grabbed his coat and Stetson and then jumped into his car. It didn't make sense, but he had to know. Didn't she have a horse that was pregnant? Why hadn't he paid more attention to her animals?

By the time he reached Lynne's house, he hoped she wasn't there and was in a hospital. But he needed to check. He needed to know. She'd apparently fallen in love with someone else and that hurt.

The house was empty, but a light was on in the barn. As he ran inside, he heard her voice. He stopped at the stall and saw Lynne and another man tending… What was that horse's name?

Lynne looked over her shoulder. Seeing her surprise, Reilly wished he hadn't come. She was perfectly fine.

"Reilly, look! Bay had her twins! Aren't they adorable? Best of all, Bay made it through. It was such a worry." She washed her hands and walked out of the stall and straight into his arms.

As she cried, he held her close. Everything was always right with her in his arms. He looked over her head at the other man. The man never glanced their way. A good sign.

"How did you know to come?" she asked as she took a step back and then wiped her eyes.

"I had one more paper for you to sign, and I wanted to let you know it was coming. A man answered and said you were having twins and you were having trouble. I asked if he was sure it was *you,* and he said yes. I was worried, very worried, so here I am, lucky not to have gotten a speeding ticket."

Her eyes twinkled. "That was John. I was delivering the first foal and having trouble with the second. He's a good worker, but occasionally gets things confused. I'm glad he did."

She tugged Reilly toward the stall to look inside. "It's a miracle. Most horses pregnant with twins don't make it. A beautiful miracle. Oh look, Bay is getting up."

Scott scooted back and then stood, leaving the stall. "That was intense."

"It certainly was. Thanks for your help. You can go back to the clinic and tell Tina all about it so the whole town will know by nightfall." She smiled.

After Scott left, she gave Reilly a rundown on all the people she employed.

"They're feeding!" she exclaimed as the two foals jammed their heads to their mother's teats.

He smiled. "They most certainly are."

CHAPTER TWENTY-THREE

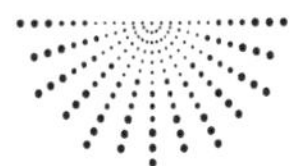

It was as if she was glowing. Such an odd sensation. But also a wonderful feeling. With a glance at Reilly, she took a sip of tea.

"I have a question. Supposing I had twins, who would you assume fathered them?"

"I had no idea, but the notion of you and another man was hard to take."

She nodded. "But you came anyway?"

"Of course. If there's the slightest chance you need help, I'll always be there. I admit I harbored a few dark thoughts about the other man." He smiled. He was so handsome.

Tears started to flow, and she quickly turned her head away. Knowing he was going to leave and go on with his life hurt beyond reason. It wasn't as though it was the first time she'd have to say goodbye.

He lifted her onto his lap, and she found herself comfortably nestled against his shoulder.

If only they could have a do over. A second chance. Yet not all wishes could be granted. Oh man, he smelled nice.

"Oh, I must smell awful!" she exclaimed. "I've been tending to horses all day, and I'm sweaty."

"You're fine. You've always smelled like a horse."

She punched him lightly on the shoulder. "I do not. In fact, I can smell nice after a shower or if I'm going out."

"Been going out a lot?"

"No. But I have had the opportunity. Many mothers here want their sons to marry me. It became a bit much turning them all down. Maybe you could do me a favor and have dinner with me in town and put a stop to the proposals?" She held her breath. What if he said no? She was a fool.

"I suppose, just this once, I could come to your assistance. I can smile and look into your eyes all evening. We could hold hands." His eyes twinkled as a smile slipped over his features. "That might give everyone the message."

"Maybe we could dance together," she added. "I'm going to take a shower. But we can't be gone long. I don't want to leave Bay alone. I'll have to ask John to stay."

"Go take your shower. I'll ask John."

"Are you sure? Just be nice, okay?" She didn't wait for an answer, hurrying away to take a shower.

Choosing an outfit became difficult. She aimed for a date-like appearance without being overdressed. Perhaps that wasn't the best idea. He was doing her a favor, but the pain when he left the last time…

She closed her eyes and pulled in a long breath. Would saying goodbye now be better or should she dance, storing the memories to warm her later? Both options were torturous, but just one more dance with him could be worthwhile.

After rummaging through her closet, she found the dress she was looking for. It was the exact blue color of her eyes.

She heard him come back into the trailer. Butterflies flitted in her stomach. Live in the moment. Thinking about the future would destroy any joy she found.

Reilly stood as she opened the bedroom door. He had his suit jacket on. Without a tie, he appeared relaxed.

Her spirits lifted at the sight of his beaming smile.

"You look amazing. Shall we? John is staying until you come home. He's a nice guy." Ever the gentleman, he opened the door and allowed her to go first and then opened the car door for her. Not many men did that anymore.

Did he sense the same powerful connection they shared?

"I'm assuming we're going to Potter's Best? I did notice two diners and Potter's Best. Been there?" he asked, beginning his journey down the road.

"I've stopped in a few times when Noreen or Tina invited me. I never stay long. Don't forget, you need to dispel the notion that I'm single and looking. I'd rather not be considered for any dates. I hope there's enough talk that it will stop all those mothers from showing me pictures of their eligible sons."

He laughed. "Has it really been that bad? I don't doubt there is interest in you. You are beautiful."

Her face heated. "Unfortunately, it is that bad. We don't have to stay long."

His nod disappointed her. Living in the moment proved more difficult than it sounded.

"They're known for their steaks," she offered.

"Of course they are. We are in Montana, after all," he teased.

It was a relief when they arrived. She'd tried to think of witty things to say, but nothing came to mind.

THERE WASN'T much of a crowd. It was more of a bar than a restaurant, but it was Potter's Best. He smiled.

"What's so funny?" Lynne asked after they were sitting at the table.

"The name of this establishment. Potter's Best what? There aren't many people here."

"Have you checked your watch? It's barely six o'clock. Give it an hour. Reilly, you're quite the handsome man. I've always thought so."

Her face turned a lovely shade of scarlet. She probably hadn't meant to tell him he was handsome.

"It's nothing I don't say to myself every morning when I look in the mirror. I make the world a prettier place."

"I wouldn't go that far. It was just a stray comment. It didn't mean anything. It's been a long day." She glanced away.

This was a mistake. There was nothing he wanted more than to kiss her, but he couldn't. Maybe if they ate quickly, he could leave.

Instead, he urged her to elaborate on her plans. And with that, dinner took a delightful turn. Her eyes sparkled as she explained everything right down to the auction she went to.

"I take it you didn't buy anything?" He grinned.

"Maybe if the items were cleaned up a bit or weren't from the last century, I may have." She laughed.

"You're happy," he stated.

She blinked. "I suppose I am. To be honest, I haven't been entirely focused on the positive. Sometimes the past edges in. The biggest difference is that people actually like and respect me. That wasn't happening in Tyrone. Sometimes I wonder if I could have done something different. Maybe I should have stood up to West. Sometimes going down that path hurts so much." She stared at him, perhaps feeling she had said too much.

"I have those moments, too. It's wonderful that you've gotten the life you always wanted. Mine is nicer in Great Falls, too."

"Wait! You live in Great Falls? When did that happen? I knew you left the ranch, but...when?"

"Remember when we met for the first time after you moved here? I told you I moved."

She wrinkled her brow. "Yes...I do remember. I'm not sure you told me where. Things were pretty emotional that day. What made you decide to move?"

A smile tugged his lips upward. "I was weary of being paraded at every corporate event as a mere show pony. No one wanted to know me. They only cared about what I could do for them, and I didn't want that. I didn't want to move back to the ranch. There isn't enough need for a lawyer there. Great Falls has been a great choice. The people are different. In fact, most know I grew up on a ranch. I work for myself and only take cases I believe in."

"You're happy," she stated, studying him with a smile gracing her lips.

THE MEAL WAS OVER, and people began to pour in. Was this it? Was this their "have a nice life, see you never" moment?

"Would you like to dance?" he asked.

It wasn't a good idea, but she nodded, her heart hammering against her ribs.

In his embrace, she relaxed, closed her eyes, and rested her head on his shoulder. For a moment, it was as though they were one. As they moved together, she felt his heartbeat and the warmth of his body. She would never experience such emotions again. She'd never been able to push him out of her heart.

The dance ended, and she pulled away. He drew her back into his arms. He didn't say a word as they danced one last time.

This time, when it finished, he let her go, and she felt a lump in her throat. She wouldn't cry. She wouldn't.

With a forced smile, she accompanied him into the cool night. Her house was only fifteen miles away.

There were no words. Gazing at his strong profile, she tried to preserve this memory.

Once more, without a word, he escorted her to the door. Before he could say a word, she put her finger over his lips.

"I can't bear to say goodbye. Good night." Quickly, she unlocked her door and went in by herself. She could no longer suppress her tears and sobbed.

The knock on the door startled her. Dashing away her tears, she opened the door.

"Are you okay?" John asked.

"Yes, I stubbed my toe. Thanks for staying. I'll see you tomorrow."

He turned and walked away.

CHAPTER TWENTY-FOUR

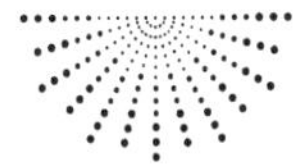

Reilly McKeegan stared at the computer screen, his mind a tangled mess. The login page blinked at him, but he wasn't seeing it—he was seeing Lynne.

Logic dictated that he should let go, that he should move on. But love wasn't logical. Neither was the ache in his chest every time he thought about her or the way his world felt hollow without her presence.

He needed her to say the words—that she didn't love him. Maybe then he could finally stop tormenting himself.

Had it really only been four days since he left Potter? It felt like a lifetime.

Enough.

Shoving back from the desk, he stood. No more over-thinking. No more waiting. He needed to see her, to settle this once and for all.

Throwing on his ranch clothes and grabbing his Stetson, he strode out the door. Maybe she didn't feel the same way. Maybe she'd moved on. But he had to hear it from her lips.

Because if she hadn't...

If there was even a sliver of hope...

Then he wasn't letting her go again.

Driving through town, his pulse pounded. Her motorcycle wasn't parked in front of the clinic. A flicker of nerves tightened his stomach. He pressed on, heading for her house.

Fifteen minutes later, he pulled into her driveway and spotted her bike.

She was home.

Reilly barely had time to step out of the truck before the barn door swung open. Lynne emerged, a bucket in her hands. Her gaze locked onto his, and in that instant, everything else faded.

The bucket hit the ground with a dull thud.

She ran to him.

Relief surged through him, and he opened his arms just as she crashed into his chest. He wrapped her up, burying his face in her hair, inhaling the scent of hay and sunshine and home.

Leaning down, he kissed her. A kiss that said everything.

How much he loved her.

How lost he was without her.

How he needed her more than his next breath.

"Lynne, I love you. Life without you is impossible. You're all I think about."

She stiffened.

His heart dropped.

He let his hands fall away, stepping back as reality came crashing down. "I'm sorry. I thought we were on the same page, but from the look on your face... I was wrong." His throat tightened. "I won't bother you again."

She didn't say a word.

His chest felt hollow as he turned, climbed into his truck, and drove away.

WHAT HAD JUST HAPPENED?

Lynne stood frozen, her heart hammering, her breath coming too fast. The weight of his words settled over her, heavy and overwhelming.

She'd waited so long to hear them.

So why had she panicked?

She staggered into her house and dropped onto the couch, pressing a trembling hand to her chest. She hadn't spoken. She hadn't said anything.

Tears blurred her vision.

She'd regret this moment for the rest of her life.

With shaking fingers, she grabbed her phone and dialed.

He answered on the first ring.

"I love you too," she whispered. "Please come back."

Silence.

"Are you sure?" His voice was raw, uncertain.

"Yes."

"I'm turning around now."

The what-ifs spun in her mind.

Where would they live? Not Tyrone. Not the McKeegan ranch. But none of it mattered. Not really.

The moment his headlights cut through the darkness, she ran outside, tears still spilling. She stood there, hands clasped, her heart in her throat.

Reilly stepped out of the truck, his face unreadable, his eyes haunted.

And she knew she'd done that to him.

She took a step forward, then another, until she was in his arms. Holding on. Never letting go.

Because this—right here—was where she belonged.

Always.

EPILOGUE

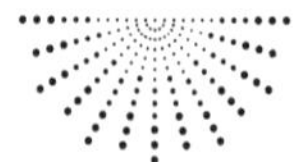

"Happy Anniversary," Reilly murmured, pressing a kiss to Lynne's lips before placing a neatly wrapped gift in her hands.

She arched a brow. "I thought we agreed—no gifts."

He grinned. "I never agreed to that."

Curious, she unwrapped the package, and her breath caught. "Oh!" Her fingers traced over the sleek *Eko CORE 500™ Digital Stethoscope*. "It's purple! And it has *Dr. McKeegan* engraved on it!" She looked up, eyes shining. "Do you know how much this cost?"

"Of course I do. I bought it." He smirked. "I had fun picking the color. Silver was too boring. But purple? That's all you."

She threw her arms around him. "I love it. Thank you."

Reilly pulled her onto the couch, tucking her against him. "I was terrified that day, driving to your house to tell you I loved you."

She smiled softly. "It was the best risk you ever took."

"I'd do it a hundred times over if it meant having you."

She hesitated, biting her lip.

He frowned. "What is it?"

"I have a present for you too." She patted the cushion beside her, her expression suddenly nervous.

"Lynne?"

She took a deep breath. "I—we—are going to have a baby."

For a moment, time stopped.

Then his arms were around her, holding her so tight she could barely breathe. "Are you sure?" His voice was thick with emotion.

"Yes."

Reilly exhaled shakily. "We are so blessed. Is the timing right for you?"

She nodded. "I've hired two more vet techs, and Robert just became a full-fledged veterinarian. I think we'll go into practice together. Our house is perfect—plenty of space for a family. And one of my biggest regrets used to be that I'd never have *your* child." Her voice trembled. "Because no one else would have ever been enough. Only you."

Emotion clogged his throat. He pressed a kiss to her forehead and whispered, *Lord, thank You for this blessing. Keep her safe. Keep them both safe. Amen.*

"We're going to be the best parents," he promised.

She leaned into him, her hand resting over his heart. "I don't want to tell anyone just yet. Not until we have to. I don't want your mother swooping in, claiming her 'first grandchild.'" She sighed. "I've thought about it a lot, and I think she actually *believes* the lies she tells. Not at first, but eventually, she convinces herself she's right."

Reilly tightened his hold on her. "I'll never let anyone hurt you again. I love you."

"I love you too."

Her eyes twinkled mischievously. "How about we go to Potter's Best to celebrate? Dance while I'm still thin enough?"

Reilly chuckled. "Sounds perfect."

And as they walked hand in hand toward their future, Reilly knew—without a doubt—that he had everything he'd ever wanted.

Everything he'd ever needed.

And he wasn't letting go.

For an extra epilogue of Reilly
https://dl.bookfunnel.com/aol25ggr0r

ABOUT THE AUTHOR

Kathleen Ball is an USA Today Bestselling Author who pulls her readers into each story. She loves to write about flawed characters and how they change for the better. Her books have happy endings, it's the story of getting there that enchants her readers.

Visit my website Kathleenballromance.com

facebook.com/kathleenballwesternromance
x.com/kballauthor
instagram.com/author_kathleenball
tiktok.com/@kathleenballromance
amazon.com/author/kathleenball

OTHER BOOKS BY KATHLEEN

Mail Order Brides of Texas set

Cinder's Bride

Keegan's Bride

Shane's Bride

Tramp's Bride

Poor Boy's Christmas

Oregon Trail Dreamin' set

We've Only Just Begun

A Lifetime to Share

A Love Worth Searching For

So Many Roads to Choose

The Settlers set

Greg

Juan

Scarlett

Mail Order Brides of Spring Water Set

Tattered Hearts

Shattered Trust

Glory's Groom

Battered Souls

Faltered Beginnings

Fairer Than Any

Romance on the Oregon Trail Set

Cora's Courage

Luella's Longing

Dawn's Destiny

Tara's Trial

Candle Glow and Mistletoe

The Kavanagh Brothers set

Teagan: Cowboy Strong

Quinn: Cowboy Risk

Brogan: Cowboy Pride

Sullivan: Cowboy Protector

Donnell: Cowboy Scrutiny

Murphy: Cowboy Deceived

Fitzpatrick: Cowboy Reluctant

Angus: Cowboy Bewildered

Rafferty: Cowboy Trail Boss

Shea: Cowboy Chance

Mail Order Brides of Pine Crossing set

Alanna

Briana

Aggie

The McKeegans

Aiden

Brayden

Myles

Caden

Nolan

The McKeegans: A New Generation

Stewart

Reilly

A Cowboy's Chance

Burke's Sweet Beloved

Clint's Sweet Calamity

Sweet Lasso Springs

Garrett

Stamos

Stetson

Sweet Cowboy Seasons

Summer's Cowboy

Autumn's Cowboy

Winter's Cowboy

Spring's Cowboy

Non Series Books

Snowbound Hearts

Spinster No More

Made in the USA
Columbia, SC
14 May 2025

57959200R00074